MY HEART WAS POUNDING in my chest. I could feel the heat radiating off the metal, and I didn't understand why.

And then a voice, an urgent whisper: *"Listen!"*

I turned and looked at Thomas. "What?"

"I didn't say anything."

"Oh. It must have been someone in the kitchen I heard." It wasn't though. I was sure of it. "I'm just a little nervous."

"Pay attention!" the voice said. This time I knew it wasn't Thomas.

I froze for a second, then remembered my mother's advice. And so I sat up straight and composed my face, determined not to show my alarm. I went on polishing in careful circles and waited for more. It didn't take long.

OTHER NOVELS BY
Diane Stanley

Bella at Midnight
The Cup and the Crown
The Mysterious Case of the Allbright Academy
The Mysterious Matter of I. M. Fine
Saving Sky
A Time Apart

The
Silver
Bowl

Diane Stanley

HARPER

An Imprint of HarperCollinsPublishers

Library of Congress Cataloging-in-Publication Data
Stanley, Diane.
    The silver bowl / Diane Stanley. — 1st ed.
        p. cm.
    Summary: From the age of seven when she became scullery maid in a
castle, Molly has seen visions of the future which, years later, lead her and
friend Tobias on an adventure to keep Alaric, the heir to the throne, safe
from a curse.
    ISBN 978-0-06-157546-4 (pbk.)
    [1. Clairvoyance—Fiction. 2. Blessing and cursing—Fiction.
3. Magic—Fiction. 4. Kings, queens, rulers, etc.—Fiction. 5. Inheritance
and succession—Fiction. 6. Fantasy.] I. Title.
PZ7.S7869Sjl 2011   2010021967
[Fic]—dc22   CIP
                                                                          AC

Typography by Adam B. Bohannon
13 14 15 16   CG/OPM   10 9 8 7 6 5 4 3 2
❖
First paperback edition, 2012

for
Nancy
and
Murray Bern

CONTENTS

The Silver Bowl

❦ 1 ❧

I Am Sent
to Dethemere Castle

I WAS SENT AWAY TO WORK when I was very young. I suppose it was not surprising. Father was poor enough already, having failed in the tailoring trade, without the added burden of a mad wife and the seven children she'd borne him. He could not possibly feed so many.

Nor did he care for us overmuch, being rather more a surly than a sentimental man. He kept Tucker on to help in the cutting room, and Anne to run the house and look after Mother. But excepting Robbie, who quarreled with Father and ran away, the rest were hired out as servants as soon as they were old enough.

Being the youngest, and of no account, I think my very existence slipped Father's mind much of the time. I was rarely at home except to gulp down some soup and curl up in the corner to sleep. Then I was off again in the mornings to run wild in the streets, where I played with the boys, and learned coarse words from them, and got into fights, and mussed my clothes, and came home with dirt on my face.

Then, around my seventh summer, I came to Father's attention. I'd been in particular trouble of late—and not for the first time, either. Of a sudden he was all on fire to be rid of me.

He thought I might find work up at Dethemere Castle. It'd been a heavy summer for plague in those parts. One of the royal princesses had died of it, and a good many serving maids, too. Surely they'd be hiring new people. They might even be so desperate as to take on the likes of me.

Once he'd decided to send me off, he couldn't wait another day. He called Anne and told her to make me presentable and to do it bloody quick: clean me up, he said, and dress me in my Sunday gown. If there was anything that could be done about my hair short of washing it, she was to do that too. We would set off within the hour.

When I was ready—scrubbed raw about the face and hands, my skirts brushed more or less clean of dust, my hair pulled back so tight my head was throbbing—I asked if I might bid Mother good-bye before we left.

"All right," Father said. "But be quick about it. Anne, go let her in."

My sister kept the keys now; Father did not go in to Mother anymore.

The room was cold, and close, and dark. I stood for a moment, blinking in the dim light, as Anne shut the door behind me and locked it again. I took a quick, sharp breath to steel my courage.

"Mother?" I said.

She was sitting on the bed, her hair all arranged; it was as if she'd known I was coming.

"Don't you look fine," she said, "in your Sunday gown, and in the middle of the week. He must be sending you away, then. What are you now, child? Six?"

"Seven. Just."

"That's young."

I shrugged. "I'm a lot of trouble."

Mother smiled at that. "Sit here beside me." She

patted the coverlet. "It hurts my neck to look up at you." She draped her arm across my shoulders; it seemed to have no weight at all. Not like Father. When he touched you, you felt it, sure.

"So tell me, little Molly—what have you done that is so troublesome?"

I licked my lips and turned my head away.

"Still fighting with the boys?"

"Yes."

"But it was something else."

I nodded.

"You can tell me. I won't be angry."

"It wasn't my fault," I said. "It just . . . happened. Now Father says there's sommat wrong with me, and I'm too much trouble, and I must go away."

"Ah," she said as if I'd told her everything. I thought she sounded sad, or disappointed. "Let me guess: you heard a voice calling to you—only there wasn't anybody there."

I shook my head. No.

"You had a vision, then, of something that was yet to be."

"He told you!"

"No, Molly, he didn't."

"Then how—?"

"I just knew, that's all. Go ahead. I need to hear it."

I put my thumb to my mouth, then remembered that was a nasty, baby habit and took it away again. "We were playing Catch the King. We only play Touch now, since Jemmy got knocked down so hard that time and whacked his head on the cobbles."

"Go on."

"I was chasing Jack, and I caught him. I touched him on the shoulder, that's all."

"And?"

I couldn't say it.

"Molly, you have to tell me."

"I saw him dead of the pestilence, Mama. Just quick-like, but it was real as can be—he was all covered with purple blotches, and his mouth was hanging, and his eyes were open but they didn't move. And so I screamed, and ran away from him, and said he had the plague. They all laughed at me."

"But then?"

"In the night he took sick, and the next day he died. Now they won't go near me anymore. They call me a witch. The neighbors are talking."

Mama closed her eyes and sighed. "Your father is right to send you away. Such things will keep happening, and people won't understand. They'll say—"

"It was just the *one time*, Mama. I won't do it any-more!"

She gave my hand a feather-squeeze. "You can't help it, child. It's in your blood. You got it from me, and I from my papa—only he was clever and knew what to do with it, and I never have. Perhaps—"

"I don't know what you mean."

"I see things, Molly, same as you. I know things without being told, and hear voices. They make me frantic sometimes." She gazed out into the darkness, and for a moment I wondered if she'd forgotten I was there.

"Father says you're mad," I said. "Are you, Mama?"

She turned and looked at me. "I don't think so. And neither are you. But people fear what they don't understand, so they think me mad and they call you a witch. Oh, how I wish you didn't have to bear this. I'd hoped it would end with me. All these years I've watched my children for any sign of . . . the *gift*, but it was never there. Except perhaps for Robbie; I did won-der about him. I guess we'll never know for sure, now that he's gone." She drifted away again, and I waited. Then, without turning back to me, she almost whis-pered, "But there's no question that *you* are one of us."

I pulled away from her, then, and got up from the bed.

"No," I said. "We're not the same."

"I didn't mean to frighten you, but I must prepare you for what lies ahead. And I'd best do it now, for there won't be another time."

"You don't know that."

"Yes, I do. Now listen to me and remember what I say: when these things happen in the future, try not to draw back in horror and surprise, or to cry out. It's natural to be frightened, I know, and it may be that you haven't the skill to hide it. If that is the case, then you must spin some tale. Say a spider bit you or that you are prone to fits. But whatever you do, don't tell anyone the truth."

I nodded.

"Because, believe me, child: this"—she gestured with her hand, taking in the dark room and the lonely life she spent in confinement there—"this is not the worst that can happen to such as us."

"Oh, Mama—"

"Anne!" I heard Father calling from beyond the door. "We need to go."

"Quick," Mother whispered. "I have something for you. Come here." She removed her beautiful necklace and hung it around my neck.

I was thunderstruck, for it was her dearest possession and the only thing of value in our house. Her papa had made it for her mother long ago: a delicate disk of silver filaments, all twining about like threads in lace, hanging from a silver chain. He'd worked their initials into the pattern: a *W* for *William*, an *M* for *Martha*.

"Don't let your father see it," she said, "or it'll wind up in the nearest pawnshop. Tuck it into your bodice. Good. Now only you shall know it's there."

"But don't you want it?"

"I've had it long enough, since I was a little child. And it has always comforted me, and given me courage, and protected me in dangerous times. Papa put some good magic into it, and . . ." She drifted away again.

"What, Mama?"

"I think that you might need it."

"Anne!" Father shouted again. "Where are you? Get in here."

"You mustn't show it around at the castle. It's not the sort of thing that servants wear. But whenever you feel sad or afraid, just touch it, like this." She put her hand to her heart where the necklace used to be. "And it will—"

I heard the key scratching in the lock; then the door opened. There stood Anne, her face solemn.

Father was right behind her, dressed in his traveling cloak.

"Time to go," he said.

⁓ ❦ ⁓

My mother died the following spring.

I'd been sent to the pigsty with a bucket of slops and had just stepped out into the yard. Suddenly all around me the air seemed to breathe a heavy sigh— *haaaaaaaaaaaa*—and in the dazzle of the sunlight I could make out my mother's face. Somehow I knew she was dying, though she didn't seem troubled at all. Quite the contrary, she looked peaceful, content, relieved, as when you lay down a heavy burden or come inside on a bitter cold night and kneel before a blazing fire. I was glad. I told her good-bye.

That was my second vision. It would not be my last.

❦ 2 ❦

The Donkey Boy

FATHER TOOK POWERFUL long strides for such a runty man. It was all I could do to keep up with him. And he never once turned around to see if I was still there.

What if I fell too far behind, I wondered—would he bother to come back?

Well, of course he would! He'd have to retrace his steps to get home. The real question was what he'd do when he found me. Thrash me senseless and drag me to the castle? Or say good riddance and leave me where I was, to starve, or be devoured by wild beasts, or be set upon by brigands?

As none of those outcomes seemed very appealing,

I galloped along behind him, gasping and panting, my scrawny legs trembling with the effort.

We spent the night in a farmer's hayloft, without the farmer's consent. Father would not pay for an inn. Then we were off again before sunrise, and late that afternoon we came to Dethemere Castle—whereupon Father offered me up at the gatehouse like a loaf of bread at market.

He told them I was nine.

I can't imagine they believed such a lie. All the same, they took me on as a scullery maid.

It was a dirty job, the lowest of positions, though I didn't know it then. I thought myself very grand to be working at the castle, a servant to the king. Oh, how I planned to lord it over Anne when next I saw her.

I never got to, of course. Father left me there and never came back.

"Mind you, behave yourself," he said. "And if they send you away, don't bother to come home."

"I will, Father. I mean, I won't, Father."

"'Cause if you do, I'll beat you within an inch of your life."

"I know you will, Father."

I was an ignorant child. I couldn't read or write. Nor had I any manners to speak of. No one had ever taught me to be pleasant, speak softly, listen patiently, and try to make people like me. My lessons had all been learned on the streets. And so I was loud, and coarse, and hasty with my fists, renowned for my cleverness with insults.

None of this was useful at Dethemere—even I knew that. I'd have to learn some new tricks, and learn them bloody quick, if I was to keep my place. And keep it I must, else I'd soon be sleeping in doorways and begging for my bread.

I was put under the charge of a big girl named Bertha, who'd worked there for several years. She enjoyed ordering me about as though she were a duchess and I was her lowliest servant. Yet she was just a scullion, same as me, except that she was trusted to handle the fine and delicate things, while I attended to the pots and the spoons, and whatever could not be broken.

On my third day she happened to go to the privy, leaving some goblets on the sideboard waiting to be washed. They were made of fine crystal, etched with cunning designs and rimmed with gold—worth a fortune I'm sure. I should never have touched them. But I thought to impress Bertha by showing how helpful

I could be. Perhaps she would be kinder to me then. And so I picked up one with my soapy hands.

You've already guessed that I dropped it.

The donkey boy was standing in the doorway. His hair was in his eyes, his nose ran, and his mouth hung open. Naturally, I took him for a dimwit. Never did I dream he could be quick.

But quick he was. He saw the goblet fall; and suddenly there he was, upon his knees, hands outstretched. He caught it before it hit the ground, lost his balance, rolled over onto his side, then onto his back, all the while holding it safely aloft. At last he rose to his feet again and handed it back to me—after which, having spoken nary a word, he returned to his place by the door.

As ill luck would have it, Bertha came back just then. She took the goblet from my hands and carefully returned it to the sideboard. Then she grabbed me by the hair and dragged me into the kitchen, where she presented me to the cook, who gave me a proper beating and threatened to send me away.

"I won't do it again," I wailed. "Oh, please let me stay! Just give me one more chance."

The cook did not answer. He just gave me a look of utter disgust, followed it with a kick to the backside, then returned to his work.

It was the best I could have hoped for.

I went back to the scullery, red faced and shaking. Bertha had finished with the goblets by then and had put them safely away. Now she was waiting, her arms crossed, her piggy eyes smoldering with rage. First she slapped me across the face, then she shoved me against the sideboard and started pulling my ears and twisting my nose. All the while she threatened me with certain death if I ever did such a thing again.

And of course I couldn't fight back.

When she finally grew tired of knocking me around, she pointed to an iron cauldron—I swear it had been used for a hundred years and had never once been washed—and ordered me to make it shine. Then she left.

I wanted to weep. No, that's not true; what I really wanted was to punch someone. Either Bertha or the cook would do. But as that was not wise, I went to work on the pot.

"Don't mind her," said the donkey boy.

I turned. Wonder of wonders, he had a voice.

"I don't," I said. "But I dare not lose my place."

"Then you'd best be careful."

I glared at him. "You don't have to tell me that."

I went at the pot with the soap and the sand. I was cross, though I had no one to blame but myself. And it annoyed me that the donkey boy just stood there, watching.

"Don't you have anything to do?" I asked.

"Not right now."

"Lucky you." I pulled my hands out of the greasy water and inspected them with dismay. My knuckles were scraped and bleeding.

"Try wrapping your hand in a dishcloth," he said. "Then the sand and the rough parts won't chafe your skin."

I stared at him.

"My mother used to do that. It's a good trick."

I dredged a cloth out of the dirty water, bound my right hand in it, and went back to work. He was right. A good trick indeed.

"You're not really a half-wit, are you?" I said.

"No," he answered. "Though I think you're the first to notice."

"Doesn't that bother you?"

He shrugged. "It's what they want me to be—stupid and strong, the perfect donkey boy."

"Why do they call you that? You don't work with donkeys, or any other animals, so far as I can see."

He laughed. "*I'm* the donkey, didn't you know? I haul and carry."

And suddenly I wasn't angry anymore.

"Do you have a real name, then? Besides Donkey Boy?"

"Yes," he said. "Tobias."

I turned the pot and went to work on a different section.

"You know, people wouldn't take you for a dullard if your mouth didn't hang open like that. Close it, and maybe they'll think you're a prince."

"I can't."

"What, close your mouth? Of course you can!"

"Not for long. Not if I want to breathe."

"That's what you have a nose for, you numbskull."

"I have a nose, but the air won't go through it. It's all filled up."

"Blow the snot out. That's what other folk do."

"I have, many a time, but it comes right back. There's something wrong with my nose, I think. I'm forever sneezing and sniffling, all through the spring and the summertime."

"Well, what if you only opened your mouth a little bit, enough so you can breathe, and didn't let it hang down so far. That might work, don't you think?"

He tried it.

"And wipe your nose when it drips. Use your sleeve."

He did.

"Brush the hair out of your eyes."

He did that too.

"See? You are much improved. Not that I would actually take you for a prince. I just said that. But maybe a young gentleman or sommat like that."

"How would you know? I bet you never saw a prince in all your life. Nor a gentleman, neither."

"Of course not."

"Well, I have."

"Chaw! You're telling stories."

"No, it's true. I mend the fire in the king's hall. Oft times the great folk pass by."

"Truly?"

"Truly."

"Then, you must take me with you. I'll help carry wood. I'm stronger than I look. I'll be your donkey girl."

"You won't get into trouble with Bertha?"

"She left. And if she comes back and catches me gone, I'll make up some excuse."

"All right, then. But you'll have to behave."

"Oh, I will," I said. "I promise."

❦ 3 ❧

The Prince

"WE MUST BE SILENT AS GHOSTS, Molly. And if one of them should come into the room, look down in a very respectful manner, and do not meet their eyes, for they don't wish to be reminded we are about."

"Why? If I had a castle full of servants, I'd be glad to be reminded of it."

"Well, they are not. We are as common as lice to them, and just as interesting."

We'd made our way down the back stairs to the service area below, where the pantry and buttery are. Against the far wall stood two long tables, placed end to end. They were for setting down wine flagons, and trays of food, and all other such things that came and went during the dinner service. Flanking the tables were a pair of doors that led into the great hall.

We went in and set down our logs on the hearth. Then Tobias went to work shoveling ashes into a bucket, while I looked around me in amazement.

"It's so grand," I said. "Bigger than our church at home."

"What did you expect? It's a king's hall."

I studied one of the tapestries. It was a picture of a gentleman and a lady, dressed in beautiful clothes, in a garden filled with flowers. They appeared to be dancing. "How would you make a thing like that?" I asked.

"I don't know. Weave it, I guess."

"How rich would you have to be to own—what is it?" I counted. "Fourteen tapestries?"

"Very rich. And they have plenty more of 'em, too, in the other rooms."

"How many people do you suppose could they fit in here? For a meal, I mean, not just standing around."

"*I don't know*, Molly. Stop asking questions. And keep your voice down."

"Sorry."

It was then that I noticed the little dog. It was so small and fluffy. I wondered if perhaps it wasn't a dog at all but some other kind of animal I'd never seen before. It had on a red collar and was scratching at a door on the side wall. It must have slipped out in search of whatever bits of food might be hidden amid the rushes on the floor; now it could not get back in.

I went over to the door, meaning to open it just a crack to let the dog go where it wanted. I heard Tobias gasp. When I turned, I saw terror on his face.

"No!" he whispered.

I pointed to the dog.

He shook his head violently. "That leads to the royal chambers!" He gestured frantically for me to come back to the fireplace.

I covered my mouth and winced at my mistake. I was just tiptoeing away when I heard voices. I couldn't help it; I stopped to listen.

"It's long past time you went," a woman said. "Edmund left when he was eight. Why is this so hard for you to accept?"

"I don't want to go, that's all."

This was spoken by a boy. I couldn't tell how old he was, but his voice had not yet changed.

"Well, you can't stay here. A castle may have one king and one heir—and you are neither. Only Matthias belongs here now. It's time you went out and became a man, and found your own place in the world, just as Edmund has done."

"By being a common page, and serving at my cousin's table, and being ordered about like a servant?"

"Every man who wishes to become a knight must do the same."

"But they are not princes of the blood."

"Oh, Alaric, you would do well to be a little less fond of yourself."

"But I don't even want to be a knight, Mother. I have no desire to ride around slashing people with my sword. And I'm not overfond of horses."

"You'd rather sit around in the garden all day reading old history and Latin poetry?"

"Yes, Mother, that's exactly what I'd like. What's wrong with it?"

"Well, if you're that fond of books, you can go into the church. It's a respectable option. You could be a bishop."

"I don't want to be a bishop. Not in the least."

Tobias was creeping toward me now, his face like thunder. I waved him away and—sorry, but this is true—pressed my ear to the door.

"You are impossible!" said the lady.

Silence.

"You must go, Alaric. Your father says so, and I agree."

"Then send me somewhere else. I will not have Reynard ordering me about. He's my own cousin, but just because he's so much older than me he acts like—"

"Alaric!" The woman was furious. "You are not his equal. Reynard is king of Austlind, and you are only a prince, and a third son at that. It is wholly appropriate for him to—"

"And I hate those disgusting bully sons of his too."

"Oh, when will you grow up? I cannot talk to you anymore!"

"Fine!" came the reply, followed by hasty footsteps.

I was halfway back to the fireplace when the boy stormed out. He left the door open, and the dog scampered in. Moments later, the door slammed shut.

But I hardly noticed any of that; I was too busy gazing at the prince.

His hair was golden, and clean, and hung to his shoulders in shining curls. He was slender and richly dressed. And his face, though red with anger, was so beautiful that I was near to swooning—till he turned and glared daggers at me.

"Mind who you look at, wench," he said, then tossed his head and strode out of the hall.

Tobias stood frozen till the prince was well out of hearing. Then he turned to me in a rage. "I cannot believe you," he said. "Standing at the king's door, listening to a private conversation! Are you completely out of your mind?"

"Everybody does it," I said. "How else can you know what goes on in your neighbors' houses?"

"You are not at home," he said. "These are great folk, and their doings are none of your business. If they'd caught you with your ear to that door, you'd surely lose your place—and I'd lose mine for bringing you here."

"I'm sorry," I said.

He finished building the fire in stony silence, then swept the hearth clean. Finally he picked up the bucket of ashes and ushered me out of the hall.

"Well," he said, his voice kinder now, "at least you got to see your prince."

"I know."

"And I'll wager you thought him the handsomest thing that ever you saw in your life."

"I did. And if you stuck him, and stuffed him, and hung him on the wall, I'd be very glad to admire him. But in life he's an arrogant pig, and I didn't care for him at all. *'Mind who you look at, wench.'* Foo!"

We were halfway up the stairs by then. Tobias stopped, and laid the ash bucket down, and took me by the arms. He was very angry.

"You aren't fit to be here," he said.

"And you are?" I said. "Snot-nosed mouth-breather."

"No. I'm humble and ignorant, same as you. But at least I respect those I serve and have sense enough to think before I speak. But you—I don't know what you are. Just stupid enough to be dangerous."

"I wasn't serious, you goose."

"You threatened the prince."

"I did not!"

"Stick him and stuff him—"

"It was a joke!"

He gave me a hard look. "You don't joke about such things."

Then he let go of my arms and, grabbing the ash bucket, stormed up the stairs. When he reached the landing, he turned and looked down to where I stood, leaning against the railing.

"You'll be lucky to last here a week," he said.

＊＊＊

He was wrong, as it turned out. I lasted there a good long time. And when I finally did leave, it wasn't because they'd sent me away.

Tobias had much to do with it. For his words

stung me as Father's whippings never had, and I set out to prove him wrong. I let him chide me when it was needed, and I didn't pull faces or call him names when he did it. In time I learned how things were done in the king's service. And so I settled in there, and was accepted, and found my place at Dethemere Castle.

❦ 4 ❧

Calamity

I SLEPT IN ONE OF the basement storerooms, along with five other maids. The place was crowded with old furniture, and piles of lumber, and barrels of salted fish and meat, and bags of undressed wool. It stank in there of fish and sheep dung.

I shared a bed with Winifred, a sweet-natured, big-boned country lass who never left off talking. I believe, if such a thing were possible, that she was even more ignorant than I was.

Until I arrived, she'd had the bed all to herself because no one wished to bunk with her. She tossed about in her sleep something awful, poking me with her elbows, sometimes driving me off the bed and onto the floor. And in truth it might have been more peaceful just to sleep down there, for all that it was hard and cold. But I had a fear of rats running over me in the dark, and nibbling at my toes, and getting tangled in my hair. And so I kept to the bed and fought with Winifred for a few cramped inches of space.

Late one night, three years after I'd come to Dethemere, there came a soft knock on the storeroom door. No one heard it but me. I was already awake, Winifred having just rolled onto her back, flinging her right arm wide, thumping the back of my head, and so I sat up in bed and called, "Who is it?"

The door opened and there stood one of the kitchen lads, a candle in his hand.

"You're all to get up and dress," he said. "You're wanted upstairs."

"Why?" Hannah asked, awake now. She was the oldest, our mother hen. "Is something the matter?"

"There's been an accident," he said, stepping into the room to give Hannah a light from his candle. "That's all I know." Then he turned to go. "Be as quick as you can."

I could hear the scuffling of his feet as he hurried down the hall, then a knock on another door and the sound of sleepy voices.

By the time we got to the kitchen, the great iron chandeliers that hung from the vaulted ceiling had been lowered, and lit, and raised again. Candles glimmered on worktables and the shutters were open wide, though the sun wouldn't be up for hours yet. Fires were already going in the grates, and pots had been set over them to boil.

In one corner a sleepy-eyed boy sat on a stool killing chickens. There was already a whole tub full. That many chickens meant a very big meal, not some common breakfast. We'd been called to prepare a feast, then, in the middle of the night.

We stood in a huddle, hugging ourselves in the cold, speculating in quiet voices as to what sort of accident it had been and who it was that had suffered it.

Tobias came in with a load of wood. I waved him over, but he only nodded and left to get more wood.

Finally one of the steward's men came upstairs to address us. He seemed impatient, as though speaking to the kitchen staff was a waste of his precious time. I noticed deep frown lines on the sides of his mouth. *That scowl must be his commonplace expression,* I thought. *Nothing to do with us.*

"Everyone, please!" he shouted. "Give me your

attention." He spoke as highborn people do, confident and loud. When we had quieted down, he began.

"I have come to inform you that Prince Matthias is dead. They're bringing his body back now, and—"

We all forgot our manners then and started peppering him with questions. He raised his hands and bellowed for silence.

"A messenger has been sent to fetch Edmund, as he is now heir in his brother's stead. Noblemen from across the kingdom will be arriving soon to pay their respects to the prince. We must provide for them as is fitting. You have a great deal of work to do."

Tobias was back now. He slipped into the crowd of servants and wormed his way through the packed bodies, heading in my direction.

"Sir, can you tell us something of how Prince Matthias died?" This from the cook.

The steward's man sighed but nodded assent. "All right," he said, "but it will have to be brief. I have many things to attend to. The prince was hunting in the king's deer park, north of Storrow Palace. . . ."

He went on speaking, but I heard nothing more of what he said. For something strange came over me. It was like the time my sister was washing my hair and she pushed my face under the water, just to be mean. I could hardly see; the world around me became a blur of shapes; and the steward's voice was like the honking of a goose, a faraway sound with no meaning.

And then I found myself at the edge of a green wood, surrounded by horsemen and dogs. I could hear the horses stirring about and the hounds whimpering, eager to be off on the chase.

I saw it before they did—a beautiful stag with enormous antlers. It stepped daintily out of the brush and into the sunny clearing, then looked warily around and sniffed the air. Sensing the hunters, it froze for a heartbeat, then sprang forward, changed directions, and darted into the cover of the forest. The hunters spurred their mounts and hurried in hot pursuit.

Now here is the thing I must tell you: I'd never set eyes on a stag before; I knew nothing of hunting. There is no way I could have imagined all that—unless perhaps I was remembering it from that day in the king's great hall when I was seven and stood there in amazement, admiring the beautiful tapestries. One of them might have been a hunting scene. But no, I did not think that was it, for this was real as real. I could smell the forest, hear the thunder of hoofbeats, and the blast of hunting horns, and the yelping of the frenzied hounds. Where could that have come from?

I saw Matthias now, riding ahead of the others, his face aglow with excitement. I'd never seen him, either, but I recognized him all the same. I admired his fine features, his broad shoulders, his rich and beautiful clothes.

That was when I noticed the peculiar vine. It hung from a tree in the middle of the path shaped like a hangman's noose. I was sure it hadn't been there before; it had just appeared out of nowhere.

Matthias saw it too and tried to rein in his horse, but he couldn't stop in time. Nor could he turn to avoid it, because the path was so narrow. So he ducked, pressing his cheek against the horse's neck. He would go under it.

That should have saved him, but it didn't because— I swear this is true—the vine reached right down and scooped him up. And so the horse went on without him, while Matthias hung there . . .

I heard myself moan and felt someone's arm around me. I looked and saw it was Tobias. His face was grave, and there were tears in his eyes; but he didn't say a word, just shook his head at the sorrow of it and gave me a kind little squeeze. I nodded silently and covered my face with my hands.

"At least they're well stocked with sons." The voice came from the back of the room. Everyone turned to see who would say such a thing. It was the pastry cook's boy.

"Shame!" came cries from all around.

"Shocking!"

"Shut your gob or I'll shut it for you!"

"I didn't mean no harm," the boy protested. "It's just—you need a prince to inherit, now don't you? And so it's good they still have a couple of 'em left. That's all I meant."

Somebody shoved him; he shoved back.

"Stop that this minute!" the steward's man roared. "You lot of lumpish swine!" He clapped his hands as though we really were pigs and he was shooing us away. "Now get to work, all of you. We must do honor to the prince and make everything splendid for his coming-home. Do you understand me?"

We did.

⤙ ⤚

As it was still the middle of the night, there were no pots or dishes to wash. And so I was put to work plucking the chickens, along with Winifred and several of the kitchen lads. Tom, the poulterer's boy—the one we'd seen killing the chickens—was going to show us how.

"Can Tobias help, too?" I asked.

"Tobias?" Tom asked.

"The donkey boy," said one of the lads, laughing. "He's your sweetheart, ain't he, little scullion?"

"And what do I want with a sweetheart, you maggot? I'm ten."

The lads burst out laughing. "You'll find out soon enough," one of them said. I felt a squeezing in my chest.

"The prince just died, you sour lumps of flesh, and you stand there making coarse jokes. You *are* a pack of swine!"

"Enough!" Tom said, disgusted with the lot of us, but he did call over to Tobias. "Donkey Boy," he said. "If you're not needed elsewhere, come and help us here. And the rest of you"—he looked daggers at the lads—"show some decent respect."

He led us to a cauldron of water then, already heated near to boiling. Beside it was the basket of birds, some of them still twitching. He gripped one of them by its big, gangly legs and plunged it into the water—a quick dip, just enough to help release the feathers but not so long that the chicken would start to cook. We all in turn did likewise, after which we carried our wet, scalded chickens over to a spot beside the window. There we sat on wooden stools and went to work pulling feathers.

It's a messy business, and smelly, too. But I was glad to have something to do. I thought that if I could only concentrate hard enough, I might drive that terrible image from my mind: the prince hanging from the nooselike vine, his body swaying, his head lolling, his red velvet cap with its beautiful plume lying upon the ground.

I shuddered, and Winifred noticed.

"It's awful, awful," she said.

"I can't stop thinking about it."

"Me neither." She shook her head sadly. "They be cursed, you know—the royal family."

"Hannah says that's a lot of nonsense," I said. "Fairy tales."

"No, it's not. Hannah just doesn't like us gossiping about it. She's such a little prig. But the girl that was here afore her—the one that died in the night—she told me all about it one time, and there's no question: they're cursed."

"I've heard it spoken of, too," Tobias said.

"All right." I kept my voice low, turning away from the rowdy lads who still watched me with smirks on their faces. "Tell us what you know, then."

Winifred paused, and pinched her lips, and leaned in even closer. She had her own way of telling stories. I was well accustomed to it.

"There was the old king, Mortimer, father of Godfrey, who's our king now; he was the first one cursed. He was desperate to have a son to be his heir;

but years and years passed, and in all that time he only got one daughter, Gertrude."

"That's not a curse, Winifred. Wives are barren sometimes."

"Three of 'em in a row, Molls?"

"You didn't tell me that part."

"Well, I am now. Three queens, side by side, buried in the chapel yard and only the one baby in all that time, and she of no use on account of being a girl."

"My father would've been glad to have that problem," I said bitterly. "He had children aplenty and didn't want a single one of us."

"But your father ain't a king now, is he?"

"No."

"Well, then. So Mortimer married for the fourth time, though by then he was very old—and sure enough, he got himself a son, quick as you please. That was Godfrey, of course."

I was beginning to think Hannah was right; it was all nonsense. "So everything was fine. Really, I don't see how—"

"Then the queen died of childbed fever."

"As women do, Winifred. All the time."

"I'm not done, Molls. I've only just started. The next thing that happened, the nurse dropped poor little Godfrey smack on his poor little head, and broke his arm and his leg; and they thought for sure he'd die. Only he didn't. He's just lame, that's all."

I looked over at Tobias. He was trying not to smile. "Nurses can be clumsy, Winifred," I said, "same as anybody else. Next you'll say the clouds cursed him by covering the sun one day."

She looked hurt. "I'll stop if you don't want to hear the rest."

"I'm sorry. Wait just a second." I tossed my plucked chicken into the basket and went to fetch another. When it was scalded, I brought it back, and took my place again, and smiled at her. "Now go ahead. I'll listen."

"All right. The next thing that happened, King Mortimer died. Godfrey was hardly much more than a boy." She looked to see if I would interrupt, point out that old people die with some regularity. But I said not a word.

"He was bit by a serpent, Molls. In winter. There was snow on the ground, icicles hangin' from the eaves."

"That's unnatural, Winifred. I'll admit it."

"It was devil-sent. Had to be. It was the curse."

"All right," I said. "Is that all?"

"No. Now Godfrey didn't have his father's curse; he's been blessed with many children. But look what's happened to them. First Princess Agnes died of the plague. Then poor Princess Elinor caught the pox, and her face was so disfigured that she goes about hiding behind a veil. And now Godfrey's heir, Prince Matthias, hung by a vine while hunting. That weren't natural neither. That vine was put there special to hook the prince."

I stared at her, my mouth agape. The steward's man had told us about the vine, exactly as I had seen it. I must have heard him tell of it—through my fit, or my fog, or whatever it was—and imagined how it looked. It hadn't been a vision, then. Most likely just a lively imagination led on by the man's story. I felt a surge of relief.

"You see?" Winifred said.

"Yes." I nodded in agreement. "I do."

"But Winifred," Tobias said, "this curse . . ?"

"What?"

"Well, how . . . how would someone go about doing that, putting a curse on a person? And why would he want to do it? And who . . ?"

Winifred sighed and gazed down at the chicken in her hands.

"Truly, Tobias," she said, "I wish I knew."

❧ 5 ❧

The Silver Bowl

WHEN FIRST I'D COME to the castle and started working in the scullery, I was so small I had to rise up on my toes in order to do my work. Now, while I wasn't uncommonly tall for my years, I had to lean over to reach the bottom of the sink.

When I wasn't scrubbing pots and washing dishes, I did whatever was needed. I swept floors, and carried slops to the pigs, and hauled water, and plucked fowl, and scoured the worktables twice a day. It was never pleasant, but I saw it was no worse than what the others had to do. So I made up my mind to be cheerful about it and finally won the acceptance of my workmates in the kitchen. That was a comfort, for I no longer had Tobias to cling to. He'd been promoted to groom in the stable yard, and though I visited him there as often as I could, he wasn't by my side all the time the way he used to be.

I missed him terribly and often thought how well he'd guided me back when I was just a rough child from the streets and he was a donkey boy. He'd taught me to take pride in my work, no matter how lowly it might be. Now when I scrubbed a pot, though it might take me an hour, it was like new when I was finished. Even the cook remarked upon it once.

Thomas, the Gentleman of the King's Silver, took note of it too. He it was who had charge of all the platters, and serving bowls, and wine flagons, and candlesticks, and standing dishes, and other such finery as was used when the king dined in the hall. Thomas saw that it was polished as needed, and until recently he'd had an assistant to do it. But the boy had been overhasty with his work and had scratched a certain handsome cup that belonged to the king in particular. He was dismissed on the spot and was never seen at Dethemere again.

Now Thomas needed someone to replace him. He'd noticed my meticulous work and thought me a likely candidate. And so he approached me one day as I stood at the sink, hands deep in greasy water.

"What are you called, child?" he asked. "What's your name?"

"My name is Marguerite, sir, same as the queen. But everyone calls me Molly."

"Well then, Molly, leave that pot for someone else to finish and find yourself a clean apron. Then follow me. I wish to see if you can polish silver."

My heart sank. I didn't want to take on such delicate work for fear that I'd lose my place as the boy before me had done. "Oh sir, I think that would be too hard for me."

"I shall judge that," he said. "Come along. Do as I say."

There was no way I could refuse. I made myself presentable, then followed Thomas to the silver closet.

It was a good-sized room, with storage chests and cabinets along three of the walls and a long table in the center. The door to the room was uncommonly stout and had a double lock. No wonder—it held a fortune in silver.

Thomas showed me how to make a paste of chalk and water—only rainwater was ever used, for it was pure—and how to grind it finer than fine.

"Now watch," he said.

He wet a strip of good linen, squeezed out the water till it was only damp, and dipped it into the paste.

"Gently," he said. "In little circles, as I have seen you do with the sand when cleaning the pots. But don't press too hard. This isn't pottage baked onto an iron cauldron. It's a whisper of tarnish on something precious and fine. Do you understand me?"

Yes, I said. I did.

Thomas handed me a candlestick. It was badly dented on one side and nearly black with tarnish. "Let's see what you can do."

I went at it with all the care in the world and soon lost myself in the work. Thomas sat and watched, his hands folded, saying not a word.

"Now you must wipe it clean and buff it," he said, showing me how to do it. I followed his lead, using a boar-bristle brush to sweep out whatever paste still lingered in the deep places of the candlestick, then burnishing it bright with a clean strip of felt.

When I was finished, I looked into Thomas's face to see how he liked my work, and indeed he came very close to smiling.

"You will do," he said. "I think you have the touch for it, and the patience, too."

At first he only gave me simple things to work on: spoons, and the little salt bowls that were used at the lower tables, and now and then a silver cup. But in time he let me polish almost anything. For though he was meticulous about counting the silver before it went out to the dining hall, then counting it again after it was washed and brought back in, and writing it all down in his little book—indeed, he seemed to enjoy these tasks—he was not overfond of polishing.

But then, it was only natural. He was a gentleman servant. He didn't need to do the work himself; he had only to see that it was done to his satisfaction.

There was just one piece he wouldn't let me touch, and that was the great saltcellar that stood in pride of place at the king's high table. The base was near a foot wide, with carved angels flying all around it and three great lions atop that holding aloft the crystal dish in which the precious salt was kept. It was a wonder, no doubt about it. And I was heartily glad he didn't want me to polish it, for it would be a terrible chore to clean. And oh my soul, they would surely hang me if ever I put a scratch on it!

There was another piece, though, nearly as fine and famous as the saltcellar; and though it wasn't as grand, I liked it better. This was the great basin over which the royal family and their special guests washed their hands in warm, perfumed water when dining in the hall. They did this before meals, between courses, and again after they'd finished eating. The ceremony required three servants—one to hold the bowl, one to pour water from the ewer, and one to carry the fine linen towel with which they dried their hands.

The bowl had come from Austlind and was made by a famous silversmith. "He died long ago," Thomas said, "but while he lived there was none to equal him. And this is almost certainly his greatest work. I doubt there's another one like it in all the world."

The underside of the hand basin, as well as its wide, flat rim, was etched all over with delicate scroll-work in the form of intricate knots, and flowers, and twining vines—birds and butterflies, too. But the inside of the bowl was the true marvel. That part was more boldly carved, deeply incised, in strange and mysterious shapes.

"'Tis most ingenious," Thomas said. "For it is here on the inside that the water is poured. And as it comes streaming in, it runs through the valleys, and jumps over the hills, and sparkles as it goes. Only the mind of a great artist would think of something like that. But it's the very devil to polish."

As I sat admiring it, the beautiful pattern began to quicken before me, transforming itself into a menagerie of strange, unfamiliar creatures; but I could not hold them long enough in my mind to see exactly what they were. In an instant they'd vanished, becoming once again only a beautiful design.

"It seems almost . . . *alive*."

"So it does," Thomas said. Then he set the bowl before me and bid me polish it.

"You cannot mean it," I said.

"I never say what I do not mean."

"No, of course not. It's just . . . the bowl is so precious and fine, and I have only been working on the silver a short while, no more than three months. What if I should scratch it or sommat like that?"

"Then you would be beaten and sent away." Then he smiled. "But I trust that will not happen, for I've watched you, and I see that you are careful and have a gentle touch. It takes wondrous patience to work the paste into every little crevice, and to brush it all out again, and polish well both the high places and the low. I have enough to do already with keeping the records and attending to the saltcellar. From now on this shall be your task."

I hung my head and trembled all over.

"Pick it up," he said. "Feel it in your hands."

I did, then set it down again, as gently as though it were made of eggshells.

"'Tis monstrous heavy," I said.

"Yes," he agreed. Then he got up, and went to a shelf, and came back with a blanket of felt. "Always lay it on this, so it won't rub against the table as you work.

I generally start with the underside. It's easier. Once that is done, you can turn it over and attend to the inside. That takes the most time."

I nodded.

"What are you waiting for?"

I closed my eyes and took a deep breath.

"Nothing," I said.

❧ 6 ❧

Listen!

I PINCHED A BIT OF CHALK PASTE between my thumb and forefinger just as Thomas had taught me, feeling for any remaining grit that might scratch the bowl. It was as smooth as butter. And so I took up my damp linen cloth, and dipped it into the paste, and began.

I started on the bottom and found it was not so different from polishing the cups, ewers, and flagons I'd been working on for months—just bigger, and more beautiful.

When I had that part gleaming bright as new, I turned the bowl over and did the rim. Then came the real challenge.

"How do I get into the deep parts?" I asked. The

cloth wanted to skim the mountaintops and leave the valleys untouched.

"Fold the cloth and use the corner to force the paste down in there," Thomas said. "See, watch how I do it. Now you try."

"Like so?"

"Exactly."

It was at this point, as I was growing more confident, that I felt an odd warmth in the silver, as if the bowl had been kept near the fire. Only it hadn't—I'd seen Thomas take it from the cabinet, and it had been cold when first I touched it.

"Is something wrong?" he asked.

Maybe I was rubbing too hard.

"No," I said, and went on, with a lighter touch this time. But the metal grew warmer still, and now I began to sense a humming beneath my fingers, as though I were touching a hive of angry bees.

"Are you sure?"

"I'll stop if you want," I offered.

"No, Molly, it's your task. I want you to continue. Only—be careful."

"I am."

My heart was pounding in my chest. I could feel the heat radiating off the metal, and I didn't understand why.

And then a voice, an urgent whisper: *"Listen!"*

I turned and looked at Thomas. "What?"

"I didn't say anything."

"Oh. It must have been someone in the kitchen I heard." It wasn't though. I was sure of it. "I'm just a little nervous."

"Pay attention!" the voice said. This time I knew it wasn't Thomas.

I froze for a second, then remembered my mother's advice. And so I sat up straight and composed my face, determined not to show my alarm. I went on polishing in careful circles and waited for more. It didn't take long.

The pattern began to transform itself now, to melt into a kind of picture: it was a room with people in it, only everything was silver; there was no color to it.

I saw a beautiful lady dressed in velvet and ermine sitting in a chair. A young man knelt at her feet, holding her hands in his. He was tall and slender, with fine, broad shoulders.

Then I heard him speak. His voice seemed to come from a distance: deep, and hollow, and strange. "I will do it gladly," he said, "whatever you ask of me. I have sworn it, and I would gladly swear it again."

"Good. You know it must not be connected to me in any way."

"Of course."

"And you will have to leave me for a time."

"I know. But not for long, surely."

"Until it's done. Then *I* shall come to *you*." She smiled as if she'd said something clever.

He leaned down and kissed her delicate hands.

"So be it."

"You always were my favorite," she said. "I sometimes wish . . ."

I smiled without meaning to. It was so sweet.

"Is something amusing?"

"No, Thomas. It's just so beautiful, that's all."

"Ah."

I went back to polishing, somewhat less frightened now. If I must have visions, it was a comfort that they be sweet ones like this.

The room was still there, and the same two people. Only the lady had different clothes on. The man did, too. So—this was a different day, another time.

The woman was standing now, a piece of paper in her hand. She bit her lip, and there were tears in her eyes.

"Oh, it's too much!" she said. "Unbelievable. Cruel."

"What does he say?" the man asked.

"He withdraws the offer—his pathetic, disgusting, *insulting* offer."

"But why?"

"Why do you think? He's been successful at last. And I always was . . . invisible to him." She fell to her knees suddenly and bent over as if she had a terrible bellyache. Then she began to wail, tearing the letter into pieces. The man knelt beside her and put his arms around her. She rested her head on his shoulder.

"Too cruel!" she said again. And then the room filled with mist, and the vision was gone.

I turned the bowl a few degrees and began to polish a new section. I had, by then, grown curious. There was a puzzle here; I was eager to make it out.

"*Look!*" It was the voice again, speaking rather more gently this time, as you might when pointing out a flower or a sunset.

Once more the pattern began to break up and take new form. Only now I was in a different place, a tradesman's workshop of some kind. There was a man in the room wearing a leather apron. He had a goodly face, square and solid, with a fine crop of hair and little wrinkles around his eyes.

He was holding a child, perhaps a year old; and he lifted her high in the air, as far as his arms would reach, so he could kiss her little toes. The baby squealed with joy and wiggled her feet. He kissed her toes again. She bumped his nose. He laughed.

Oh, that was lovely, I thought as the vision faded. I shifted the bowl again, dipped my cloth in the paste, and went on with my work. The fear had left me entirely now. I was eager to see more. The bowl did not disappoint me.

"Now," said the voice. *"Watch!"*

I was back in the workshop again, only at a greater distance this time, so I could take in the whole room. I saw fine silver pieces laid out on the shelves. A silversmith, then—perhaps the one who'd made this bowl. The man was still there, though the baby was not; and he seemed to be looking straight at me or just over my shoulder. I almost turned to see if there was someone behind me, but I knew nobody was.

"You don't think it a marvel?" the silversmith asked.

"That isn't the point," someone answered. I couldn't see who it was. "It's not what we asked for."

"You wanted a splendid gift for a royal prince."

"Don't toy with me. You know the child was meant to die."

I flinched.

"What?" Thomas asked. He was still watching me.

"Nothing," I said, still holding my gaze. "Just an itch." I scratched my neck and went back to my polishing.

"We were most specific. Why could you not get it right? We certainly paid you enough."

The silversmith didn't answer.

"You will make us another, a cup this time. Do it quick, and do it right."

"No. I've done enough already." He pulled a leather bag out from the pocket of his apron and dropped it onto the worktable. "It's all there," he said. "Every farthing. You get the bowl for free."

But the bag lay where it was, untouched.

"We made a bargain. You gave your word."

"That's true. You asked me to put curses in the bowl—or rather you demanded it, upon pain of death. And so I gave them to you, as I said I would. A hundred, to be exact."

"What—the clumsy nursemaid? You call *that* a curse? So what if the boy's lame? He can still grow up and have sons. That was trifling, insignificant, worthless. And where are the other ninety-nine? The child is blooming like a rose, despite the limp."

"I never agreed they would be lethal—though you apparently failed to notice that. I was very careful as to what I said, for I am a man of my word. And the nursemaid, by the way—that had nothing to do with me."

"In that case, I can't see that you've given us anything at all."

"Oh, but I did. And I counted them carefully, every one: stub a toe, slip and fall, hit your funny bone, bump your nose, lose a toy, skin your knee, cold porridge. Infant curses for an infant child. And I put in a Guardian, too, a sort of kindly schoolmaster to look after the curses and make sure they behave."

"How terribly clever of you." The voice was as cold as ice.

"I thought it was, rather. I bought myself some time to get my family to safety. And I only did a very little harm."

"Was it worth dying for?"

"You think to surprise me, but I knew from the start that my life was forfeited. You'd never let me live with what I knew. I'm surprised it took you this long to come back. By the way, that fellow you hired to watch me—you might not want to use him again. He was terribly obvious. And when my wife went off to the market with the baby in her basket, he followed *me* to the apothecary."

"We'll find them."

"No, I think not. I feel quite sure of it."

He knew he was about to die; I could see it in his face. But he refused to cower or plead for his life. He straightened his shoulders and looked at his enemy, dignified, defiant.

Kick him, I thought. *Don't give up! Run!* But two strong hands reached out to encircle the silversmith's neck, thumbs pressing on his windpipe.

I couldn't watch it anymore. I let out a groan, and dropped the cloth, and buried my face in my hands.

"What?" Thomas cried. "What have you done?"

I shook my head.

He leaned over and studied the bowl, searching for any damage.

"I'm sick, that's all. My guts are churning, and my head spins."

He looked at me hard, then picked up the bowl and set it down at his own station.

"I'll finish it for you this time, but you need to get over your fear. It's childish, and I won't have it."

"I think I'm going to vomit," I said.

"Well, for heaven's sake, Molly, go and do it someplace else."

❧ 7 ❧

A Little Spot
of Madness

NEVER IN MY LIFE had I taken to my bed because I was feeling ill. Father had no patience with sickness. We were expected to carry on, no matter what.

All except Mother, of course. But none of us wanted to be like her.

I remember once when I was very small there was something wrong with my ears: they pained me something awful, and my cheeks were hot with fever. But I never mentioned it, and for sure I didn't linger at home. I went instead to the tanner's house, which seemed a very grand place to me then. Certainly it was large and had a wall around it, and inside that wall there was a garden.

That's what I was after: the shade from the trees.

I sat at the edge of the street on a clump of rag-gedy grass, leaning against the tanner's wall. My feet rested in the gutter—never mind that it had rained that morning and water was running over my shoes, carrying its usual burden of filth. The water was cool and the shade a comfort. I slept there for hours and did not wake till almost dark. Only then did I make my way home, where I got a lashing for spoiling my shoes.

I didn't cry. Even then I was tough as old leather.

And so it astonished me how alarmed I'd been by what I'd seen in that vision—me, the girl who never took fright. But then this was murder I'd witnessed, and a plot against a royal prince, not some street fight or a whipping from Father.

I hurried through the kitchen as though Thomas had sent me on an urgent errand, then raced down the side stairs and through the hallway into the storeroom where I slept at night. I shut the door behind me, and got into my bed, and covered myself with the blanket.

I don't know how long I lay there curled in a ball weeping myself out, but it felt like hours. At some point I grew too exhausted to cry, and for a time I actually slept. When I woke I felt a little better, but my eyes itched and my head was throbbing. I sat up, wrapping the blanket around me, and leaned against the wall trying to concentrate, determined to make some sense of what had happened.

Infant curses, I thought. *That's what he'd said: stub-a-toe curses.* Only it wasn't true. People in the royal family were dying, not losing their toys or hitting their funny bones. Oh, you could explain away Agnes and Mortimer's queens. Lots of people died of the plague. Lots of women died in childbirth. But what about Mortimer and that snake in winter? What about Matthias and the nooselike vine?

I began to feel overwhelmed again. I had to get up and move. And so I went over to the pile of undressed wool in the corner—large bales of it, bound in canvas and strapped with ropes, one stacked on top of the other. I gave it a hard kick, then did it again and again. Finally, worn-out and panting, I sat back on the bed, laid a hand to my heart, and took a great, deep breath.

I felt my mother's necklace, hiding under the bodice of my gown. I fished it out and held the disk in my hand. It warmed to my touch, as the bowl had done— only instead of seeing horrible visions, I felt a thrill run through my body. It was like a cold drink on a sultry day, unexpected laughter, sweet music, a gentle touch on the cheek. . . .

My mind cleared. I could think.

All right: the voice in the bowl had spoken to

me—the Guardian, it must be—but not so far as I knew to anyone else. Thomas had seemed so puzzled when I'd smiled unaccountably and then when I'd been so troubled. If it had happened to him, even once—if the metal had grown warm, and tingled and hummed to his touch; if a voice had commanded him to listen, then showed him a vision—he'd have known what was wrong with me. He'd have said, "So it happened to you as well?" or sommat like that.

No, the Guardian had fixed on *me*—wanting to tell me about the curse and how it all began. What's more, it apparently thought I could do something about it.

Me, of all people!

I went back in my mind to Winifred's story, the sad history of the royal family; and as I considered it carefully, it appeared to me that the Guardian had been doing his job, at least for a while. After the nursemaid had dropped the baby—which the silversmith said was none of his doing—nothing more had happened for years. True, the queen died; but as I said, death after childbirth was common. Little Godfrey grew up, lame but healthy. Then the winter-snake bit old Mortimer. Godfrey was near grown by then. So from the time the bowl arrived at the castle till the first unnatural death—what was it, thirteen, fourteen years? After that, another great span of time went by. Godfrey grew up, married, and fathered five children. Then they grew up too. How many more years was it—fifteen, twenty—before Prince Matthias died?

When Winifred told her story, it had sounded like a string of cursed events; but really there were only two over a long, long span of time.

Suddenly I felt much better. Something had gone awry, that's all—perhaps the Guardian had fallen asleep and the curses had just slipped out. Or maybe the silversmith made a mistake: one or two of the curses turned out to be stronger than he'd intended. You could hardly blame him. A hundred curses was a lot to keep track of.

But if everything was under control, why was the Guardian sending me those urgent messages?

I slipped Mother's necklace back under my gown, then washed my face, and dried it on the coverlet, and went in search of Bertha. Maybe she had some pots I could scrub.

I would not go in search of trouble. If it wanted me, it knew where I was to be found.

❦ 8 ❧

More Calamity

THE HALL WAS ABLAZE with torches and candles. By the time we arrived, a crowd had already gathered there. Many were gentlemen, knights and priests and such. But there were common folk from the village, too, and servants such as us. Some were whispering among themselves, but mostly they stood in silence, facing the king's chair of estate with its canopy of cloth-of-gold. But no one was sitting there. Nothing had happened yet.

We'd been roused in the dark of night, just as before, when Prince Matthias died. Only this time we were told to dress in our best and come posthaste to the hall. Having rushed, we then waited for more than an hour. Now and again more people would arrive, and the crowd would press ever more tightly together in order to make room for them. I kept looking around for Tobias; but there was such a crush, and I was so hemmed in by others who blocked my view, I could not find him anywhere.

Then I felt a hand on my shoulder and saw that he was behind me. He was always doing that, appearing out of nowhere.

"This way," he whispered, taking my arm and guiding me through the crowd to a spot near the wall. We could see better from there.

"Have you heard anything?" I asked. Working as he did in the stable yard, he was likely to know. For anyone important who came in or went out of the castle would of necessity pass his way to fetch a horse or to leave one.

"An outrider came in a few hours ago and roused the stable lads. Said there was a great contingent of court gentlemen on the way, and we must be on hand to see to their mounts. That's all he said. When the gentlemen arrived, they had somebody in a wagon. Ill or wounded. But he was all wrapped up, and they wouldn't let us near the wagon."

"You couldn't see who it was?"

"No. They told us to get out of the way and attend to the horses. Then they carried the man inside."

"It has to be someone important. Why else would they make such a fuss and call us here in the middle of the night?"

"Yes. Someone in the royal family. . . ." He looked down thoughtfully.

"What, Tobias?"

"Only two of them are away from the castle right now. The king, who is hunting, and Alaric, who's living in Austlind."

I felt a stab of grief at the mention of Alaric. I couldn't imagine why, as I had not liked him that day in the hall. But only he, of all the royal family, had I actually seen face-to-face. He'd spoken directly to me, though unkindly, and I'd listened as he sparred with his mother the queen, and he had seemed so unhappy. It was as if I knew him just a little.

"Look," Tobias whispered, squeezing my arm.

The door to the royal chambers opened, and the queen came forth, followed by six gentlemen. They were carrying a litter.

"It's the *king*!" came whispers all around us.

They set down the litter on a trestle table and propped up King Godfrey with pillows. He looked very ill.

"My people," the king said. His voice was weak, and all in the room strained to hear what he would say. "I have called you here to say my farewell, for I am sore wounded, and there is no hope that I shall recover."

The crowd groaned, though they could not have guessed it was anything less.

"So that there shall be no loose talk, I wish you to know that it was no man who dealt me this mortal blow but a wild beast."

Later we would all get to see that terrible creature; its body was hung from a pole on the ramparts till the birds and the bugs had picked it clean, down to its misshapen bones. And I can tell you for a fact that it was a monster, not like anything in nature.

"Hear me say this yet again: *no man did me harm.* Indeed, those who were with me came instantly to my aid and killed the beast, and bound up my wounds, and brought me here so I might die as I wished, cared for by my good wife and shrived by my lord archbishop.

"Edmund," he called. The prince stepped forward and knelt before his father, bowing his head. He was near as handsome as Alaric, I thought. And indeed, when he later became king, he was known as Edmund the Fair. But that night he just looked pathetically young, his shoulders too narrow for the burden that was being laid upon them.

"Hear, all of you, and know my last desires: that

Edmund shall rule after me, as is proper, he being my oldest living son." As he said this, the king laid his hand on Edmund's head, like a blessing.

Then Godfrey made a gesture and the archbishop came forward, flanked by two priests, each holding a holy relic in a beautiful case made of crystal and gold. They glittered in the torchlight. I could not see what was in them, but it was surely something important— the toenail of a saint, perhaps, or a vial of the blood of Christ, or a fragment of the holy shroud.

"I ask all my knights to step forward," said the king.

He waited. It took some time. There were many in attendance, and those who'd arrived last and were in the back had to make their way through the crowd. At last they all stood before him, their heads bowed.

"In the presence of these holy relics"—here the priests held the golden cases high, as they do with the host during Mass—"I ask you, every one, to swear the oath of peace. Put away your grievances toward one another, whatever they may be, for civil war is a despicable thing."

He coughed feebly and gasped for breath, but was determined to go on.

"We suffered under it before, when Mortimer died and left me to rule—a boy, and a cripple, too.

There were those who thought me unfit to be king and wished to take my place. And many here lost fathers and brothers in the fighting. It was needless, and wrong, and it must not happen again. Edmund is my lawful heir, according to tradition and the laws of this land. You must pledge to protect him, and support him in all things when I am gone."

The knights dropped to their knees and most solemnly swore to do so. Then they returned to their places, and all grew quiet again.

"As Edmund will have the kingdom and all that goes with it, I give to my youngest son, Alaric, the title of Earl of Browen, with the great estate and lands that go with it, and the furnishings and livestock, as well as the village and its peasants, free or bound, and all they pay in rents and taxes so that he may live as is seemly for the son and brother of kings."

"To my daughter, Elinor, I give that which is in her dower chest, as well as her dower lands, and another box of jewels and gold coins that her mother has in her keeping, for her own use after she is married."

Elinor curtsied. As her face was covered by a veil, we could not see her expression; but I thought I saw her hands trembling.

The king now turned to Edmund again and asked him to protect his mother, to allow her to stay on at

Dethemere and not send her away to her dower estate alone and far from those she loved. In a loud voice, Edmund promised to do so.

Then the king bid the queen to come to him so that he might kiss her good-bye. She went over to the litter, and fell to her knees, and most pitifully begged him to forgive her for any wrongs she might have done him in their life together; and he likewise did the same. Then they embraced and exchanged the kiss.

After that, Godfrey laid his head back on the pillow, and closed his eyes, and shuddered with pain. The queen gave a sign, and the litter was lifted and carried back into the chamber.

"He won't last long" came a voice from behind us. "They say he was sliced from groin to armpit." I turned and saw it was an old man who spoke. He crossed himself and turned away.

I walked with my roommates back to the storeroom, where we undressed and returned to our beds. We'd be needed in the kitchen before daybreak, but while the king still lived, we were allowed a few hours' rest.

I lay there, my back against Winifred's, glad of her comfortable warmth. I wondered if Godfrey would die that night and whether the coronation of the new king or the funeral of the old one came first.

Shortly before dawn the room grew colder. I felt a gust of wind, then heard a *whoosh*, as when a raven flies close by. I knew what it was: the spirit of Godfrey the Lame leaving his crippled body and rising untethered to his heavenly rest, where he would feel no pain anymore and could walk as well as any man.

Perhaps, like the angels, he could fly.

Though I am not much inclined to praying, I put in a word for Edmund—that he might go on to be a worthy king and bear his sorrows well.

I'm sorry to say that it did him no good.

❦ 9 ❧

There Is to Be
a Wedding

EDMUND, NOW OUR KING, had for many months been
negotiating with the distant kingdom of Cortova. To
seal an alliance between the two countries, he was to
marry the king's only daughter.

And Princess Elinor, Edmund's older sister, had
been betrothed since before her father's death.

But neither of these weddings could take place
until Westria had mourned the death of Godfrey.
And so, for the span of one year, no stately dinners
were held in the hall. Music and dancing were banned
throughout the kingdom, and all the court went about

dressed in mourning drab. Even servants such as we wore armbands of black cloth. We spoke in hushed voices as if fearing to wake the dead.

Now the year was over and we could proceed with the business of the living. And so Elinor's wedding was set for two weeks after Michaelmas. Not long thereafter, at Christmastide, Edmund would marry the princess from Cortova.

After such a long season of gloom and sorrow, this lifted our spirits mightily—as spring does when it comes after winter's drear days. Preparations for two royal weddings would mean a lot of work for us, but there followed a stupendous reward: the house servants were all invited to attend the wedding feasts.

"You lie!" I squealed when Hannah told me this.

"Mind your tongue," she said. "I never lie. It has always been so at Dethemere Castle."

"But that is wonderful!"

"It is most generous, yes. But mind you," she added, "Elinor's wedding will be a simple affair. Not only out of regard for her father's memory, but because she doesn't much care to show herself. She is a modest lady, and solemn, and quiet."

"And then there's the matter of the bridegroom." We all turned to Sarah, who was grinning wickedly, her eyes wide with amusement. She'd not been at Dethemere long, but she always seemed to know what went on beyond our narrow boundaries.

"What about the bridegroom?" we all wanted to know.

"He's a disaster. The third son of an earl, without fortune of any kind. What little he inherited when the earl died, he wasted it all on gambling."

"No!" Winifred cried. "Why would our princess marry such a one as that?"

"Nobody else would have her."

"Why?" I asked. "Because her looks are ruined?"

"No. I don't believe that for a minute," Hannah said. "Many a lady who was marked by the pox has gone on to marry well. And Elinor is of noble blood, and has a generous dowry and great connections. There should have been highborn men aplenty who'd be glad to wed her, no matter how she might look."

"What then?" I asked.

"It's the curse."

"That again? Oh, Winifred."

"She's right," Sarah said. "All the kingdom is talking of it. First Matthias dies, then Godfrey. And such peculiar deaths they suffered, strange and unnatural. People say the royal family is under some terrible enchantment. Who would want to join them, then, however great the riches and honor?"

"I think that's very sad," I said.

"Yes, it is," Hannah agreed. "So we must do all we can to make sure everything is splendid for her wedding, simple though it may be."

And so the preparations began.

Now don't let words such as *simple* and *modest* fool you as they did me. The humblest royal wedding would stagger the imagination. The very best tablecloths were all taken out so the laundresses could wash and mend and press them. Those that would be used on the high table were given special care. Ten-inch strips of fine lace were sewn along the outer edges. It took five seamstresses more than a week to do it.

The rushes in the great hall were removed. Then all the nasty things that lay beneath them—from rotting food and spilled wine to dried vomit and dog's droppings—were swept up, after which the floor was washed. Then new, clean rushes mixed with flowers and fragrant herbs were laid down.

Carts and wagons came and went daily, bringing all manner of provisions to fill up the storerooms—mackerels, eggs, mustard, flour, salt, honey, and capers, not to mention bushels of hay and oats. Fruits from the orchards were carried in, and bounty from the fields. Over in the dairy they were making double the ration of butter and cheese, while the bakehouse turned out loaves both night and day. All manner of livestock was brought into the yard—cattle, and sheep, and pigs, and ducks, and geese, and swans—and temporary pens were built to hold them till they were slaughtered. For soon the castle would be groaning with guests, and all of them needed to be fed.

Thomas and I, of course, had to polish everything. He brought out silver I'd never seen before, pieces that were used only on great occasions. There was so much of it, and some so badly tarnished that we even brought in Winifred a few times to help with the commonplace things.

But I didn't mind the extra work. Indeed, I was glad to be in the silver closet at such a hectic time, for it was quiet in there, and orderly, and clean—so much more pleasant than the hot and steamy kitchen, where everyone went about sweaty and greasy, overworked and snappish, and orders were bellowed from first light till well after dark.

I measured the passing of time by how much we had accomplished. As each piece of silver was polished, Thomas would check it off his list. I liked to ask at the end of the day, "Thomas, how many have we finished?" He would open his book and read out what he had written there: "We are done with all the flagons, Molly. Of the trays, we have polished seventeen, with twelve more to go. Of the goblets . . ."

And so it would go. As each day passed, more and more was checked off; less and less remained for us to do. One day soon Thomas would make that last little check mark. Then the work would be over and the fun would begin.

I would have been happier, though, if I wasn't so worried about Tobias.

He'd been sent with a wagon to the king's western vineyards to bring back wine for the banquet. I knew it was a long way there and back, but a week had passed since he left and still he had not returned.

I'd gone over to the stables the evening before to ask when he might be expected. The lads there made light of it and winked at me knowingly. Why did everyone think we were sweethearts? I wrinkled my nose at them, and they laughed.

"It may be he was set upon by brigands." This from Morgan, the tall one.

"Or savaged by wolves," suggested Willem, a red-faced fellow with pustules on his cheeks and a sad little mustache on his lip. "They've been seen in great numbers about these parts, hunting in packs. Everyone has remarked upon it—the other carters and the guests who have lately arrived."

"You're not funny," I said. "Not in the least."

"Oh, take a joke. Don't be an old prune."

"I'm leaving," I said, and turned to go.

I was near across the stable yard when Willem called after me. "It's true about the wolves," he said.

And so you will understand why I was uneasy and distracted. As I worked, I ran down a list in my mind of possible delays: muddy roads, high water, a bridge down at a river crossing, a lame horse, a loose wheel. Such things could happen to anyone. And Tobias was sensible; he'd know what to do.

I finished the tray I'd been working on and handed it to Thomas, who wrapped it carefully in linen and returned it to its accustomed place. Then he took up his pen and checked it off.

I said I needed to visit the privy before I started on the next piece. Thomas nodded, and I left the room.

That had only been an excuse, of course. What I really wanted was to look out the kitchen windows. I could see the stable yard from there; I hoped to catch sight of Tobias and put my mind at ease.

I didn't see him, though I spied the next best thing: a wagon piled high with casks, newly come into the yard. Of course those casks might be filled with oil—or beer, or mackerel. But I chose to believe they held wine from the king's western estates. My heart lifted.

Then I returned to the silver closet, and there at my place sat the great silver hand basin, waiting for me to polish it.

I looked at Thomas pleadingly. I had not touched the bowl since that first terrible time. And though Thomas had been most displeased with me, he'd agreed to do it himself—for a while, he'd said, till I'd mastered my fear. Now, apparently, that time had come.

"No nonsense," he warned, before I uttered a word. "The hand basin was to be your responsibility; I'm not going to do it for you anymore."

"Oh, Thomas, I beseech you. Let me polish anything else. I'll even do the saltcellar if—"

"No, you will *not*!" he said. "You will do as you are told or I shall find someone else who will. Truly, I used to think you a sensible girl, but you've become as silly as any—"

"All right," I said, sitting down at the table and picking up the polishing cloth. "I'm sorry. I won't complain anymore."

Still I hesitated. I put down the cloth again and tested the paste between my fingers. I had just been using it five minutes before, and it had been perfectly fine. But I pretended it wasn't quite right, and added a few drops of water, and ground it again with the pestle.

Thomas gave a little sniff of exasperation. He could tell I was stalling, and he was nearing the edge of his patience.

I would work fast, I decided. It would be over in a trice. The bowl wasn't very tarnished. So I fixed my face in the usual mask of concentration, dipped my cloth in the paste, and began. I took my time with the back of the bowl. It had never given me any trouble. Then I turned it over and finished the rim. Now there was no help for it; I must endure whatever the bowl had to show me.

Soon I felt the tingling beneath my fingers. The silver began to grow warm. How long before the voice would start telling me to listen, to pay attention, to—?

"Listen!" it said. *"Pay attention! There is not much time."*

As before, the pattern began to grow misty and melt before my eyes until gradually an image was revealed. It was blurry at first, as when you look at the world with tears in your eyes. But quickly it settled and sharpened.

By the light of a candle, I saw the hands of an old man. He held a quill pen; nearby was a bottle of ink. He was writing something. I heard the pen scratch as it moved across the paper and the soft breath of the writer as he worked. Now and then he wiped the tip of the pen with a cloth, then dipped it into the ink again.

Ha! I thought, and almost smiled. *Write all you want; I'm as ignorant as a pig. I can't even read my own name.*

But no, I was not to be let off that easily. For now there came the same familiar voice. It was going to read the letter to me!

"'It is to my everlasting shame that I have failed you, my beloved, that I've bungled matters and kept you waiting all these many years. But at last our forces, which slept for so long, are awake and growing in their power.'" *Scratch, scratch.* Wipe. Dip. "'The tragic events that have occurred of late tell me this is so. Surely they will not pass up this incredible opportunity, with all the family gathered at a single table!'" *Tink, tink*— dipping the pen into the ink again, tapping it against the neck of the bottle to knock off any excess. "'How it gladdens my heart to know that you shall be here to see it. . . .'"

I drew in a sudden breath. They were going to strike at the banquet! That must be what the writer meant: "all the family gathered at a single table." They planned to kill them all in a single afternoon!

"Oh, for heaven's sake, Molly!"

"What?" I said, trying to look surprised.

He grimaced, making an *O* with his mouth, furrowing his brow.

"Do I look like that?"

"Yes, you do."

"Well, I didn't mean anything by it. Honest. It's just that I've been staring at silver day and night till I'm near to going blind."

"I understand," he said, though he did not sound as if he meant it. "And you may go as soon as you're finished with the bowl. I'll be in conference with the steward for the rest of the afternoon. We'll start again early tomorrow and finish the rest."

"Thank you, Thomas."

I had scarcely touched the bowl again when the pattern began to dissolve, taking its new shape before my eyes. I was in the silversmith's workshop again, and the square-faced man was there. Standing beside him was a young woman, probably his wife; she held the baby at her hip.

These visions were confusing. They came all jumbled up and out of order. Of course this would have to be something that happened before the silversmith was killed.

"You should have refused him," the woman said.

"I couldn't. I had no choice."

"Of course you did. You might have told him you

have not the skill to do it, that you are nothing but a charlatan and your Loving Cups are a fraud."

"They're not."

"Oh, you and your silly pride."

"Listen to me: if I'd told him I couldn't do what he asked, then he would have killed me on the spot, as I'd be of no use to him and he'd fear that I might talk. Once I was dead he'd have gone after you and the child—"

"But you cannot lay a death-curse on a newborn baby, no matter the cost. 'Tis wicked, William, truly."

"I know that, and I don't intend to do it. But as long as he thinks I am willing, we will gain some much-needed time."

"Time for what?"

"For you and Greta to go somewhere safe. They'll be watching us, but I have a plan. You visit the market every day. As soon as I have made all the arrangements, you will simply not come back. Meanwhile, I shall make them a marvel, and swear that it is cursed. When it's done I'll slip away and join you."

"Oh, William—do you really think they'll let you live once you've given them what they want?"

"They might. Who can tell? If I seem compliant, they might just keep a close watch on me in hopes of using me again."

The baby had been playing with her mother's gown. Now she reached up and took hold of something with a pudgy little hand.

"Don't, Greta," the woman said, carefully peeling away the fingers.

I saw it then—the necklace. I would know it anywhere. It hung, even then, around my neck.

❦ 10 ❧

Ribbons

I SAT IN THE SHADE of the blacksmith's shed waiting for Tobias. He was helping to unload bales of hay from a cart that had just come in. But he knew I was there. He'd come as soon as he could.

I didn't mind the wait. Indeed, I was glad of it, for I was forming in my mind what I would say to him and was finding it hard to do.

I ran through truths and half-truths, even considered outright lies. I was still thinking when Tobias came over, grinning as though he'd just heard a joke— or was about to tell one.

"Molly!" he said, sitting beside me cross-legged.

"Willem says you've been over at the stables asking after me. He thinks—"

"I know what Willem thinks," I said, "and Willem is a pig."

Tobias laughed.

"I am glad you're back," I said. "Truly, I was worried. You were so late in coming."

"We didn't drive straight through. We stopped for the night."

"Because of the wolves?"

"There was talk of wolves, yes, but we didn't see any. And I never believed that story anyway. In a hard winter they grow hungry and roam in packs. But they're no danger at harvesttime. The fields are full of mice, and rabbits—"

"Tobias, I must tell you something."

"All right," he said.

"There's a plot to murder the king, and all the royal family."

His eyes went wide. "Lower your voice," he hissed. "By the saints, that is dangerous talk."

"I'm not plotting it myself, Tobias. I'm trying to stop it."

"I understand. But all the same . . ." He looked around to see if anyone was close enough to hear. But no one was, and the din that came from the blacksmith's shop was enough to drown out our words. "Who *is* plotting it?"

"I don't know." I said. "I never saw his face. But he's not alone. There are others in on it too. Several times I heard him say *we*."

"Where did you hear it? In the kitchen? That should give you some idea who—"

"No." I buried my face in my hands. There was no way around it. I would have to tell him.

"Listen, Tobias, I have a secret. I trust you to keep it. I've never told anyone before."

He cocked his head and squinted his eyes. "All right," he said.

"Sometimes I see things. Visions-like. And later they turn out to be true."

"And this plot you overheard—that happened in a vision?"

"Yes."

He lay back on the ground, his hands behind his head, and stared up at the sky.

"There is a silver bowl," I went on, "the king's great hand basin. Whenever I polish it, a voice speaks to me. And then it shows me pictures. 'Tis like a mummers play, Tobias, only dark and ugly. The man whose face I could not see, he ordered this silversmith to make the bowl—this was long ago, when the late King Godfrey was born. The silversmith was famous for these magical Loving Cups he made."

"I've heard of them—your sweetheart falls in love with you the minute the cup touches her lips. I always thought it was a fairy story."

"Well, it's not. And the bowl was supposed to be magical, too, only not like the Loving Cups. In fact, quite the opposite: it was filled with a hundred curses. Then the man sent it as a baby gift to little Prince Godfrey. He was meant to die, Tobias! And that would be the end of the house of Westria, as there would be no one left to inherit."

"That's unspeakable." He was up again, staring at me.

"The silversmith didn't want to do it, but they threatened to kill him, his wife and child, too. He needed time for his family to escape. So he agreed to make the bowl, and he filled it with a hundred curses—because he'd given his word that he would. But he tricked the man, you see. What he put in there were infant curses: piddling hurts like scraping your knee. And he put a good spirit in there too—a Guardian he called it—to keep the curses under control."

"This is most fantastical, Molly."

"I know. Do you believe a word of it?"

"I'm trying to. But I don't understand how these little curses—"

"Something went wrong. The curses got stronger. They killed old King Mortimer, then Prince Matthias and King Godfrey. Now they intend to murder the rest. And they're going to do it at the banquet tomorrow. I know because I saw the man write it in a letter. He said what an incredible opportunity it would be, with all the royal family of Westria gathered at a single table—"

"A *letter*, Molly? You cannot read."

"I know that. But the voice read it to me. It wants me to know, Tobias—the bowl, or the good spirit that lies within."

"But why you? If there is a plot against the king, would it not be more useful for this voice to tell the captain of the guards? Or the king himself, for that matter."

"Of course. And I've been wondering about that since it first began. But today I learned the reason: it calls to me because the silversmith, the man who made the bowl, was my grandfather."

He didn't speak for a minute. Then finally, "How do you know?"

"The names, for one thing. I didn't pick up on it at first, as Williams are so common. But the baby was

called Greta, same as my mother. And that's not all."
I pulled my necklace out from under the bodice of my
gown. "I got this from my mother. She told me her
father had made it. In the vision, the silversmith's wife
was wearing it."

"Oh."

I slipped it back under my bodice. "So will you help
me?"

"Of course I will." He rubbed his chin, looking
away in thought. "What is their plan? What exactly
will they *do* at the banquet?"

"I don't know."

"I mean, will they come in with an army? Or hide
assassins with daggers among the guests? Or poison
the king's wine?"

"I told you, Tobias, I don't know."

"Then how can we make a plan to stop them?"

I just shook my head.

"Well, I suppose we can watch for anything that
seems amiss. If the voice called you, it must believe
you have the power to help."

"Then it must know something I do not."

"We could tell someone about it."

"Oh, Tobias, how would that sound: I saw it in a
vision? They'll think me mad at best, and a witch at

the very worst. For sure they would never believe me."

"No, you're right. What if you say you overheard someone speaking . . . that wouldn't do, would it?"

"They'd want to know who I heard, and where, and when. . . ."

He sighed. "We'll just have to keep an eye out at the banquet. Watch the king like a pair of hawks, and the crowd, too. If something suspicious happens—"

"What? What can we do?"

"We could shout a warning."

"That's true. It's better than nothing."

We sat quietly together, feeling hopeless.

"Oh!" Tobias said, reaching into his bag. "I forgot. I have something for you. It's only a bit of frippery I got at a country fair; we passed it on the way to the vineyard."

He brought out a couple of blue ribbons, somewhat rumpled, and laid them in my hand.

"Oh, Tobias," I said. "You went to a fair and spent your pennies on me? You should have bought something for yourself."

"Why? What would I buy?"

"I don't know. Sweets."

"I wanted ribbons. I thought they'd look nice in your hair."

I felt tears spring to my eyes as I looked down at my little gift—a small thing, really, but proof that affection and kindness were still abroad in a troubled world. I broke down entirely, then, and wept like a fool.

"You're welcome, Molly," Tobias said.

❦ 11 ❧

A Wonderful Evening

I DRESSED IN MY NEW TUNIC, the one the king had given me in the spring. (He gave clothing to all his dependents, not only me. It was part of our keep, along with food, and shoes, and bedding.) I had put mine aside for just this occasion and had not worn it yet. It was nothing out of the ordinary, just a servant's gown made of coarse stuff, allover the color of dust. But at least it was clean and didn't reek of the kitchen.

I'd washed my hair the night before. Now Winifred offered to arrange it for me. She was the oldest of seven girls and knew sommat of plaiting hair. She gave me two fat braids, right at the temples, weaving the ribbons into them as she went and tying the loose ends with a bow. Then she stood back to admire her handiwork.

"Will you look at that!" she said. "How is it I never noticed afore? You're a perfect beauty, you are—and not just on account of the ribbons, neither."

"Nonsense," I said. "My own father told me many a time what a homely brat I was."

"Well, you must have grown out of it, then. That sometimes happens. What about your necklace—aren't you going to wear it, take it out from under your bodice so folk can see it?"

"What necklace?"

"Oh, come on. No use pretending to me, you goose. I seen it when you're getting dressed and such. A fine little silver circle hanging on a chain."

"Oh," I said. "My mother gave it to me. She said I was to keep it hidden, as it isn't seemly for someone of my station to wear such a thing."

"Well, not for every day, no. She's right about that. But if you'd told her you was going to a king's banquet now, I betcha she'd say different."

"I don't know."

Winifred put her hands on her hips and looked at me square on. "What's it for, then, if not to look pretty? Eh?"

For comfort, I thought. *For remembering. For protection. Good magic to balance out evil.*

She still stood there, head cocked, watching me at my thoughts. "Truly, Molls," she said, "it's not that hard a question."

I felt for the chain at the back of my neck and gave it a gentle tug, lifting the silver disk out from where it lay warm against my heart.

"You're right," I said. "I shall wear it."

~ ❧ ~

As soon as we'd finished dressing, we went up to the kitchen and joined our fellow servants. We would be given instruction on how to behave, after which we would all go down to the hall together and be seated before things got started.

We waited in the alcove, near the silver closet, so as to be out of the way of the kitchen staff. They were frantically putting the final touches on the first-course dishes, arranging things on the serving platters, saucing them as needed and garnishing them with herbs, or lemon slices, or apples, or flowers.

I noticed that the door to the silver closet was ajar. Thomas must have been in there, finishing up his accounts. He noted down every piece that ever went out of that room. Later, after the banquet, he would do it all again—checking in every platter, every flagon, every bowl as it came back. If so much as a spoon went missing, Thomas would know it.

Now here he came, locking the door, heading in our direction. And oh, my stars! He wore a black velvet doublet embroidered all over with silver and pearls, and dove gray silken stockings, and pointy black slippers topped with fluffy bows. Framing his face was a fine lace ruff, and on his head was a velvet cap embellished with a silver gray plume!

This was not the Thomas I knew, the quiet man who dressed so modestly and never called attention to himself. Indeed, at times I tended to forget he was highborn, and not some common servant as the cook was.

"Thomas," I said. "You are a wonder!"

"As are you," he said. "Little Molly, all tricked out with ribbons."

I touched my hair and blushed.

"And what have we here?" He'd noticed the silver disk. "May I see it?"

I held it up so he could have a closer look.

"Silver filigree," he said. "Child, this is a very handsome piece."

"I know. My grandfather made it a long time ago."

"Your grandfather worked in silver? How amazing.

Perhaps you were destined to work with it too." He smiled. "I see there are initials here, woven into the design."

"Yes. The *W* is for *William* and the *M* for *Martha*. Those were my grandparents' names."

"Ah," he said, and released the disk so that it dropped very delicately back onto the front of my gown. "Well, it's a beautiful piece. You're most fortunate to have it."

I nodded, but he had already turned away. He would be off to the king's chapel now to see Elinor wed. Then he and the other noble servants would begin the procession—up the grand stairway, and through the great double doors, and into the king's hall for the banquet.

Thomas had nearly reached the staircase landing when he turned back and winked at us, gracing us with a dazzling smile.

I could scarce believe it: ordinary, fussy old Thomas had been miraculously transformed that day. As he stood there in his beautiful clothes, with that expression of joy upon his face, he looked for all the world like a young man in love.

"It's going to be a wonderful evening," he said.

⟨ 12 ⟩

The Wedding Banquet

ALL THE SERVANTS WERE PLACED near the entry doors, the least desirable seats in the hall. We were as far from the king's table as it was possible to be and right beneath the musicians' gallery, so it would be noisy as well as drafty.

But no one seemed bothered by any of this—for were we not in the great hall, at a table draped in snowy linen, with silver spoons and salt dishes set out before us, soon to dine on wonderful dainties? Would we not eat white bread that day and drink real wine in the presence of our king?

I wish I could have enjoyed it as the others did. But my spirit was far too heavy. For this would not be the wonderful evening that Thomas had promised. It would end in tragedy, which was grim enough. What made it worse was that I had been warned, and I knew not how to prevent it.

I glanced at the next table over, where Tobias sat with the other grooms. He'd been watching me, waiting till I turned his way. Now he gave me a little nod of encouragement. I nodded back, then returned to my troubled thoughts.

Hannah reached across the table and slapped my hand. I'd been nervously chewing at a hangnail. "That's common," she said. "You mustn't do it here."

I blushed, and put my hands in my lap, and lowered my eyes.

Oh, how I wished I could warn the king so at least he might double his guard and be on the alert. But even if I *were* permitted to speak to him, it would sound too ridiculous: "Excuse me, Your Majesty, but I keep having these visions when I'm polishing your hand basin, and in one of them I saw this man writing a letter. And though I don't actually know how to read . . ."

Foo! They'd have my head before I even got that far.

"Molly!" It was Hannah again. "Whatever is the matter with you? Will you stop squirming?"

"Sorry," I said.

"Be still."

And I *was* trying to be still when a horn blared above us and I nearly pitched off the bench. As I was not the only one who'd been startled, Hannah let it go.

The great entry doors swung open now, and the first of the guests came in. These were the king's noble servants: the game warden, the master of the hounds, the bee ward, Thomas. They were followed by the lesser gentry, and finally the lords and ladies of highest rank.

They were like enchanted beings in their deep scarlets and forest greens and midnight blues, all interwoven with thread of silver or gold, glimmering like jewels in the torchlight as they came. They wore velvet and silk brocade trimmed with fur and feathers and pearls, gold netting and embroidery. There were slashed sleeves showing bright-colored silk underneath, and parti-colored hose, and steeple-caps as high as a five-year-old child draped with silken veils as fine as spiderwebs.

None of them looked like assassins.

Then came another fanfare, and we were all directed to rise. For now would come the greatest of the great, those who would sit in the place of honor up on the dais. The herald announced their names as each of them entered the hall: the Lord Archbishop, the Lord Grand Steward, the Lord High Chamberlain, and other such lords I have forgotten.

Then, "The right high and excellent King Reynard of Austlind!" announced the herald. "And his lady wife, Queen Beatrice!"

They came sweeping in, their heads held high, dressed alike in emerald green and gold. Oh, what a handsome couple they were, so elegant no one need be told that they were royalty. You could see it in the way they walked, in the richness of their dress and the expressions on their faces.

"The noble Prince Rupert, eldest son of King Reynard of Austlind!"

"The right excellent Prince Alexander, second son of King Reynard of Austlind!"

"The most esteemed Prince Ambrose, third son of King Reynard of Austlind!"

Three sullen princes followed their regal parents. It was clear they did not want to be there, had no interest in the wedding of some aunt they hardly knew. Most likely they'd begged to stay behind in Austlind—to hunt in the park or do whatever it was that young princes did for fun.

That was just a guess, but I'd seen my share of snotty boys over the years. I'd bet a year's wages I was right.

"The most excellent lady Gertrude, queen dowager, sister to our late sovereign, King Godfrey of Westria, and widow of the late esteemed King Osgood of Austlind!"

Gertrude was old and as thin as a post, but you could tell she'd been a beauty once. Her skin was still fine, whiter than white, set off by a velvet gown the color of blood. Like Reynard and Beatrice, she didn't bother to look about her to see the impression she was making. I suppose once you've been a queen you're quite beyond that sort of thing.

There was a brief pause, followed by another loud fanfare, longer and grander than before. It would be the royal family of Westria now.

I made a quick scan of the room but saw nothing amiss: no furtive movements of hand to dagger, no furrowed brows, no shifty glances—just a sea of bright, expectant faces turned toward the door. And so I turned that way, too.

"The noble and mighty Prince Alaric of Westria, brother of King Edmund, our sovereign lord! The greatly beloved queen dowager, Marguerite, mother of King Edmund, our sovereign lord!"

Ah. He was just as handsome as ever; his hair still curled about his shoulders with the glimmer of spun gold. But he had sprouted up like summer wheat, and his face was all angles and bones. He was more man than boy now.

I remembered that day when I was seven, when I'd listened at the queen's door—how angry they'd been with each other. And so I was glad to see them together now, the prince so attentive, cradling her arm, walking as slowly as she needed to, looking into her face from time to time with sweet concern to see that she was all right.

Oh, Alaric, I thought, *well done!*

The music began again, only now it was not just a fanfare. All the instruments were playing: pipe and lute and harp and viol, together with the horns.

"Lord Henry Hubert of Mockington and his lady wife, Princess Elinor of Westria, sister of King Edmund, our sovereign lord!"

"Oh, dear," Winifred said, gasping and hiding a smile behind her hand. And she was not alone in this—for here came the princess, a tiny, birdlike thing nearly drowned in silk and velvet, and beside her the ponderous bridegroom, short, red faced, and fleshy. His lower lip hung down, his legs were like sausages, and perched upon his pendulous nose was a wart the size of a bean.

They reached the dais now. We watched in horrified fascination as a page helped the princess step nimbly up, then offered his arm to Lord Henry Hubert. The bridegroom leaned so heavily upon the boy that they almost went tumbling down. But another page came quickly to the rescue, and between them they hauled the fellow up.

At last the couple, ridiculous and sad, took their places of honor, and the final fanfare began.

❦ 13 ❧

Visions and Voices

"HIS ROYAL MAJESTY, our dearly beloved sovereign lord, King Edmund of Westria!" the herald called out in a booming voice. "And the gracious and most esteemed Princess Anna Maria Elizabetta of Cortova!"

There was a tremendous buzzing of excitement in the hall, for all were eager to see the famous princess. She had only just arrived, having traveled many weeks to get here. Now she would stay on at Dethemere till Christmastide, and her wedding to Edmund.

If he lived till then.

"Oh, isn't she fine?" Winifred whispered, poking me in the arm. "But she's not like our ladies, now is she?"

"No," I said.

"Darklike. And that hair, black as soot. And what a great, long nose she has!"

"I like her nose," I snapped. "It's better than the mushroom that grows on *your* face."

"Aw, Molls, that was harsh. I didn't mean no harm."

"I know, Win. Me neither. I'm sorry."

They were passing close by us now, all the servants gazing at Anna Maria Elizabetta—admiring her large, dark eyes; her olive skin; her glossy hair; her exotic headdress of gold, and emeralds, and pearls. That is why no one noticed me—how I sat recoiling, my mouth agape, my eyes open wide with terror. For I was looking at *him*, not her. And Edmund—oh, horrible!— was covered all over in blood, with horrid gashes about his throat. Yet he continued to walk, stately and calm, as though nothing at all was amiss. I had to cover my mouth so as not to scream.

I knew it wasn't real, not yet, anyway. But it would happen. My visions were always true. And this one— oh, I had been warned it would come at the wedding feast, with all of them gathered at a single table. . . .

I closed my eyes against the terrible sight. When I opened them again, Edmund had taken his seat at the high table, in his chair of estate, his face as handsome and unblemished as ever it was before. I watched as he leaned over and spoke to the princess. She turned her head slowly, as though she wasn't quite sure what he'd said. Then understanding dawned, and a bright smile lit her beautiful face.

Now there came another fanfare, and the banquet officially began. Out came three pages dressed in the king's livery, bringing forth the hand basin, the ewer, and the linen towel.

And that's when it struck me—what a simpleton I'd been! There were no assassins hiding among the guests. No man would rise up and slay the king with his sword. Edmund's death would come in some mysterious way, through evil magic, just as the others had. And that bowl, packed and humming with evil curses—

Already it was too late. Edmund was holding his delicate hands over the great silver basin.

I froze and watched—but nothing happened. No fire spitting dragons rose up out of the water. Lightning did not strike. The king just washed his hands, and dried them, and returned to his conversation.

I glanced over at Tobias again. His face was blanched white. He'd been thinking the same thing as I had. We exchanged weak smiles of relief.

Then the archbishop rose and said grace, after which the music started up and a procession of waiters came in. They entered the room through the two service doors, one on each side of the great gilt screen that spanned the far end of the hall directly behind the dais.

First there came the pantler, who brought out the bread and butter. Kneeling before the high table, he cut the upper crusts from the loaves and gave them to the king and his guests, after which the pantler's boys served the rest of us.

Next came the butler and his assistants, bearing the beautiful silver flagons, heavy with wine.

And finally the food was brought out, one dish after the other, each consisting of some sort of fowl, for this was the theme of the first course: Birds of the Air. We had heron, partridge, snipe, plover, and woodcock—roasted, crisp, and beautiful. There was a pudding made from neck of swan, and bits of chicken bathed in cumin and cream, as well as tiny humming-birds stuffed with dates and mustard seed, covered in wine sauce.

"Aren't you going to eat?" Winifred asked. "'Cause I'll take yours if you don't want it."

"Eat your own," I said.

"I was only asking. You can take bigger portions, you know."

"We have three more courses to go, Winifred."

"I know. I seen 'em in the kitchen: Creatures of the Sea, then Beasts of the Field, then Sweet Dainties, and Fruits, and the Tray of a Hundred Cheeses. But you can still take more if you want."

"Well, I don't."

About an hour into the banquet, the waiters came out and cleared the serving dishes. Now it was time to rest our stomachs for a while and enjoy the first entertainment. I knew what it would be; I'd seen it being constructed in the kitchen.

Above us, in the musicians' gallery, harps and viols began to play—sweet music for lovers, appropriate for a wedding. From behind the great screen there came a troupe of tumblers, followed by a chorus of village girls. They were all dressed in white and were carrying pink roses.

The children curtsied to the king, then to Elinor; and one by one they offered her their flowers. For a brief time she was nearly hidden behind a mountain of roses. Then the waiters came and moved them to the sideboard.

Poor Elinor, I thought. She could not possibly love her new husband. I doubted she even liked him. They'd scarcely met before that day; and he was old, and gloomy, and peculiar looking—and everybody knew he'd only wed her for her fortune.

Yet they were bound to each other for life. Soon she'd have to leave her childhood home, the great castle of a mighty king, to dwell in some middling hall such as an earl's youngest son would have, most likely stripped of all its great hangings and best furnishings to pay off his gambling debts. And there she would run out her days, sitting alone behind her veil, doing needlework by the fire—

Blast those trumpets! Was there no end to fanfares?

Ah, they were bringing in the spectacle: a pie so enormous it was carried on a cart drawn by a pair of dwarves dressed as little lambs. And bringing up the rear of this charming procession was the pastry cook, his garb gleaming white, even to his spotless apron.

He bowed low before the high table and asked if they wished him to serve up the pie. There were smiles all around, for of course everyone longed to see what was inside.

I already knew, yet I felt uneasy. Everyone and everything that came near the king might be suddenly transformed into something else. Something deadly. I shot a warning glance at Tobias.

The cook took out his long knife and carefully cut the top of the pastry—first one way, then the other, in the form of a cross. Now he stepped back as two heads emerged: it was another pair of dwarves, dressed as a bride and a groom. The little woman wore a circlet of rosebuds on her flowing golden hair.

While the guests were still applauding, the tiny bridegroom disappeared into the pastry shell again. Then he popped back up and, raising his hands to the rafters, released a flock of snow-white birds. The birds circled the hall in great confusion, trying to find their way out.

Now it was the bride who disappeared. The music swelled, and when she stood up again she was holding a wee infant. Oh, how everybody laughed when the cook cut open the sides of the pastry and the couple stepped out and walked around the hall bidding all to admire the child.

While servants ran in to clean up the mess and roll the cart away, the village girls finished the entertainment by singing country songs, all about love and marriage, while the little "lambs" danced and frolicked around the hall.

A few of the guests left their seats and headed in the direction of the high table. I leaned forward, on edge. But none of them went anywhere near the king; they left the room through the service doors.

Ah, I remembered—the latrines were at the top of the stairway. I saw Alaric touch his mother's arm, excusing himself to do the same.

And heaven help me, it did cross my mind—a stray thought, for only a second—that I could follow him there on the pretense of wishing to use the privy myself. I would get to see the prince up close, perhaps even speak a word to him. "Good afternoon, my lord prince," or sommat like that.

Of course I didn't do it.

And thus I was still there in my seat by the door when the terrible thing happened.

❦ 14 ❧

The Terrible Thing

"DO YOU FEEL THAT?" I asked Winifred. "A draft?"

"No," she said, fanning herself with her hand. "It's hot in here, Molls—all those torches and candles. I'm sweating like a hog."

I didn't know what to make of that. I definitely felt a current of air, so cool it made me shiver.

Maybe the cook had opened the windows upstairs. But that wouldn't explain it, for a breeze couldn't travel all that way to the hall if it had no way to go out. I glanced over at the entry doors; they were still closed, as they had been this last hour and more. And the only windows—high above the tapestries along one wall— were fixed and did not open. Yet, if anything, the draft was growing more pronounced, and the air wasn't cool anymore. It was bitter and sharp, like a winter wind.

I am sometimes so slow to understand things. But finally I did: it was another sign, another warning, sent only to me. And it meant that the thing would happen soon, any minute now.

I half rose. I don't know what I thought to do—shout perhaps. But then I fell back onto the bench again and grabbed the table with both hands to steady myself. For I had seen it again, only this time it was worse: King Edmund lay upon the floor, right in front of me, covered in blood as before—only now, standing over him, was a huge silver wolf. It was tearing at his throat. I moaned and covered my eyes, but even then the vision would not go away.

I was making a spectacle of myself, I knew that, and so it did not surprise me when Winifred grabbed my arm and squeezed it tight. But then I heard other people screaming and took my hands away from my face.

The doors were open wide now—and there upon the landing stood a pack of enormous silver wolves, just like the one I'd seen in my vision. They were hunched down, muscles tense, as animals do when they're about to spring. Then the lead wolf leaped across the threshold and into the hall, and the rest of the pack followed.

In no time at all they had reached the dais. All around me, terrified guests were desperately trying to escape, nearly trampling one another in their efforts. But I stayed where I was, frozen with horror, as the lead wolf bound onto the high table, and from there to King Edmund's throat.

"This way! Quick!" It was Tobias, of course—he was always there when I needed him. He guided me into the crowd that flowed through the open entry doors. We had nearly reached the landing when I suddenly remembered.

"Wait!" I said, grabbing him by the sleeve. "We have to go back."

"Go back? Molly, there's nothing we can—"

"For Alaric," I said.

His mouth hung open. He stared at me. Then he finally understood. "Let's go," he said.

Unaccountably, Winifred followed us. I couldn't imagine why. She didn't know what was really happening, why Alaric was in special danger. But follow us she did, as we fought our way through the crush of people, scrambling past overturned benches, stepping over the occasional silver platter or fallen tablecloth, always staying close to the wall and as far as possible from the snarling wolves and the carnage up on the dais. Eventually we reached a point where the flow was in the other direction, moving toward the service doors. After that the going was easier.

At last we made it through, and now the crowd spread out—sprinting up the wide stairway, streaming like a swarm of ants in the direction of the kitchen. We ran with them; but when we reached the landing we turned the other way, down the narrow hall to the left, the one that led to the latrines.

That's when we saw Alaric, just coming out of the privy, hastily rearranging his clothes, a look of confusion on his face.

"This way, my lord," Tobias said, roughly grabbing the prince's arm and pulling him farther down the hall.

Alaric seemed about to protest, but he never got the chance, for the cries on the stairway turned to shrieks of horror. We looked behind us, and there was the wolf-king, just rounding the corner, his silky fur stained and matted with blood.

To this day I sometimes see it in my dreams so that I wake up moaning and soaked with sweat: I see the wolf spring as it had in the hall, its jaws open wide, its yellow teeth gleaming and as sharp as blades. I hear the fierce growl as it falls upon the prince, going for the throat but missing it by inches, sinking its teeth into the shoulder instead, rocking its horrible head back and forth as a dog will savage a rabbit.

Then Tobias grabs the wolf's thick fur just below the ears and slips his fingers into a corner of the animal's mouth, yanking the skin back hard at the cheek so that the wolf rears back in pain, snarling and letting go of the prince, who tumbles to the floor. The wolf tries to turn upon Tobias now, but it's still being held from behind, wild with rage, snapping and writhing about.

No one comes to help us. A few glance in our direction as they reach the landing, then hurry away toward the kitchen.

It's then that I notice the prince's dagger, still at his right hip, encased in its sheath. I run forward, and pull it out, and drive the blade into the beast—but the knife strikes a rib and only enrages the wolf more. It twists its body this way and that so that Tobias loses his balance and falls, taking the wolf down with him. I fear the wolf will get the better of him soon, for the creature lies right on top of him now, rocking back and forth, trying to turn its body around to go for the kill.

But its belly is exposed.

Now, Molly! I pounce like a fiend, never mind the raking claws that slash my arm as I strike; and this time the knife bites deep. But the creature continues to struggle, pumping out blood, twitching, until finally it goes limp.

Tobias still lies there, holding tight, making sure that the thing is really dead. Then he finally gets up, stumbling a little, and slams the carcass hard against the wall.

He is panting, trying to get his breath.

Then I remember the prince, who lies insensible on the floor, his doublet torn at the shoulder and soaked with blood. I am wondering what we should do to help him when I hear more screams, louder even than before. I turn to see the rest of the wolves, the whole pack of them, standing on the landing, looking around, getting their bearings. Then they see Alaric, and their yellow eyes narrow. They are creeping toward us.

Quick as ever, Tobias leans down, and takes the prince up in his arms, and runs heavily off to the far end of the hall, calling sharply for us to follow him and to make haste. I look around for Winifred and find her huddled in a corner by the privy.

I pull her to her feet and tow her along behind me after Tobias.

We run down a stairway that leads to a storeroom below. At the bottom there is a door.

"Open it!" Tobias shouts. His hands are full, holding the prince. "Hurry!"

I slide past him, praying it isn't locked, and take hold of the latch. The door is heavy, but it opens. We run through, shut it behind us, and set the bolt.

Just in time.

The pack is howling on the stairway outside. I hear them scratching wildly at the door, throwing their bodies against it. We stand in the darkness, terrified.

That is the point where I always wake up—which is strange, for the story continues. Indeed, it has scarcely begun.

⚜ 15 ⚜

The Water Gate

"**WHAT NOW?**" I asked.

"We'll go out the water gate."

"What's that?"

"The big door over there—it opens onto the river. They bring freight in by boat sometimes and load it directly into the storeroom. We can go out that way."

Tobias set the prince down gently onto the floor.

"I can't swim," Winifred said. Her voice sounded small and high, like that of a little child.

"Nor can the prince," Tobias said. "Not in his condition. But we won't need to. They usually keep a skiff here."

"Can't we just stay in the storeroom, Tobias?

We're safe now. And who can tell what danger lies out there?"

He raised the latch and opened the heavy door. The sun had already set, but there was still enough light for us to see. Outside was a stone landing and beyond it a goodly space, a bit of the river enclosed by high walls, with a big iron grate sealing it off. It was like a room, except that the floor was all water.

As Tobias had hoped, a large, flat-bottomed skiff was tied up at the landing.

"But what about that?" I said, pointing to the iron grate. "Won't it be locked?"

"Yes," Tobias said. "I need to find the key."

"I think we should stay where we are," I said again. "It's not good to keep moving the prince about. It'll make his bleeding worse."

"No," Tobias said, feeling along the wall near the door, searching for the key. "We need to go."

"Why? The wolves can't get in. Sooner or later they're bound to go away."

Thump, bang. They were still throwing themselves at the door, wild with rage.

"Ah," he said at last. "Here it is."

"Why won't you answer me, Tobias? Why go out on the river in a boat when we're perfectly safe down here?"

"Because we're not safe," he said, pulling me toward the door. He was a bit rough about it, I thought, and hasty, too. "We need to hurry."

He pushed me out onto the landing.

"Get into the boat, now. Hold my hand till you're standing firm. Try to step into the middle if you can."

I did as he said, and felt the boat rock beneath my feet.

"Are you steady?"

"I think so. I don't like it."

"All right then: sit. Let go of my hand, Molly."

Next he helped Winifred in. She's a big, gangly girl, and none too graceful. When she stepped into the skiff, I thought for sure we would capsize, and fall into the water, and be drowned. But once she sat down on the bench across from me, the boat began to recover.

"I need your help now," Tobias said. He was kneeling on the landing, the prince in his arms. "Take his legs, Molly, under the knees. That's right. Winifred, help me lower him into the boat. Careful. Support his head."

Just then we heard a loud crash coming from inside. Tobias snapped his head around and stared into the darkness of the storeroom. Then he let go of the prince, all unexpectedly, so that Alaric fell quite heavily into Winifred's arms.

"What was that?" I said. But Tobias didn't answer.

He was frantically untying the ropes. As soon as he had the boat free, he pushed it away from the landing, then dived in himself, nearly tipping us over and crushing poor Winifred.

I heard a snarling behind us then—and there they were, coming out onto the landing, flashing their yellow teeth. How was it possible? They had broken down a locked and bolted door made of solid oak and reinforced with iron.

But then, of course, these were no ordinary wolves. I only hoped that demons couldn't swim.

Tobias used an oar to push us far away from the landing. Now he stood, clutching the bars of the grate with one hand while fitting the key into the lock with the other. At last there came a click as the lock released. He had only to swing the grate wide and we would be free. But it was heavy; as he pushed against it, we began to slip back toward the landing.

"Here," he shouted, handing me an oar. "Hold us in place."

The water in the enclosure was shallow, with a bed of stone below. I plunged the oar in till it hit bottom, then held it firmly there, keeping us from drifting back.

"Good," he said, and continued to push on the grate.

Winifred let out a moan. I turned to see one of the wolves crouching low, eyes squinted, muscles tensed. Seconds later, it sprang.

I moved without thinking, pulling my oar from the water and holding it in both hands like a club. As the creature came flying at us, I swung the oar hard. I came near to losing my balance and tumbling out of the skiff, but for that moment at least I was not afraid. Indeed, I was most satisfied by the loud *whack* as the oar struck the wolf and by the sight of the animal, dazed and bleeding, struggling in the water.

The others flew into a frenzy now; and I was ready for the next one, standing in a wide-legged stance, the boat rocking beneath me, the oar over my shoulder. But Tobias gave one final shove, and we were through the opening and out upon the river, the night wind cooling our faces. I sat down.

Tobias was a strong rower, and we were moving with the current. In time the shouts and screams from the castle completely faded away, and the distant lights of the torches seemed but fireflies hovering over water.

Only then did I remember the prince. I dipped my apron into the river and dabbed his face with cool water.

"Molls!" Winifred said, "there's nothing the matter with his face. Don't you think we ought to look at his wounds?"

"I wouldn't know how to treat them, no matter how bad they are. And we've nothing to treat them with. No bandages, or medicines, or anything."

"Let's have a look anyway. Best to know what we're up against."

"All right." I slipped down beside him on the floor of the boat. It felt improper to touch the prince at all, let alone undress him. But as it had to be done, I unfastened the handsome brooch that secured his cape and handed it to Winifred, who pinned it to her gown for safekeeping. Then I began to undo the many tiny buttons on his doublet.

"Oh!" I said, drawing breath when at last I pulled it open.

Winifred leaned in to see.

"It might not be as bad as it looks," she said. "The blood has soaked his shirt, but the wound may not be so large as all that. You'll need to take off the shirt to tell for sure."

"Do you know anything of physic?" I asked, struggling with the ribbons that held his shirt together at the neck. It was quickly growing dark, and the moon wouldn't rise for hours. Soon it would be impossible to make out anything at all.

"I know sommat of herbs," Winifred said. "I learned it from my mother. I can treat snakebite, and rashes, and fever; and I can make purges, and—"

"What about treating wounds, Winifred?"

"I know sommat of that too."

Tobias stopped rowing then and turned to look at us. "How bad is it?" he asked.

"Don't know. I can't get this blasted ribbon untied. The knot is all wet with blood—"

"Just tear it, you eejit," Winifred said, slapping my hands away and reaching down to do it herself. I heard a grunt, then a rip, and the shirt was open.

"You've ruined it," I said stupidly.

"Where's your head, girl? It's already ruined. It's soaked with blood and chewed up by a wolf."

But I was no longer listening to her, for I was studying the wound. It was hard to see much for all the blood. Every time I wiped it clean, more came oozing out.

"He's still bleeding."

"Of course he is," Tobias said. "It's only been a little time. Even a prince cannot heal that fast."

"Let me have a look." Winifred knelt on the other side of the prince and peered at his bloody shoulder.

"Aye, it's a real mess, ain't it? A couple of really nasty gashes there what need to be stitched up. Fold your apron, why don't you, with the cleanest part out, then press down hard. That'll slow the bleeding some."

I thought this sounded wise and did as she said.

"Will he die of it, Winifred, do you think?"

"Most likely not. Though you can never tell with these things."

"You have a lot of experience with 'these things,' then?"

She shrugged.

We continued to float silently down the river with the current.

"We need to find him a leech or a wisewoman," Tobias said. "There's little gain if we save him from the wolves only to have him bleed to death on the river."

"True enough," I said, "only I don't know any leeches or wisewomen, not here nor anywhere else."

"My mother is a wisewoman," Winifred said. "I told you that already."

"No, you didn't. You said she taught you sommat about herbs. It's not the same. Every housewife knows a thing or two about—"

"Hush, Molly," Tobias said. "Let her speak. Is your mother truly a wisewoman, Winifred? Or only—"

"No, she's a real one, all right. Even highborn folk

sometimes call her to their bedsides. She can all but raise the dead."

"All right, then," Tobias said. "How do we get there? Is it close to where we are now?"

"Close enough," she said, pointing downriver. "Past Oughten, past Kerrig, then just a little ways more."

"Inland, Winifred, or on the river? I shall have to carry him, you know."

She gave a joyful little snort.

"'Tis right on the river," she said.

❦ 16 ❧

The Wisewoman

THE PRINCE DID NOT WAKE until morning.

While he'd slept, Winifred's mother had looked after his wounds, treating them first with bishopswort and egg white, then stitching up the gashes that gaped most horribly with a common bone needle and thread. When she'd done all she could, she bound his shoulder with clean bandages, then waited beside him for the rest of the night, feeling his forehead now and again for fever.

Through all of it he had lain insensible. From time to time he'd moaned and moved a little, but he never once opened his eyes, nor showed any sign that he knew what had befallen him.

Now he woke to find himself on a straw pallet on the floor of a dark, smoky cottage—undressed to the waist, covered in bandages, and throbbing with pain.

"Where am I?"

He asked this of me, for mine was the first face he saw.

I'd been there since daybreak, giving Winifred's mother a chance to rest. Behind me were two little girls, Winifred's youngest sisters. They'd been there for a while already, gazing in wonder at the sleeping prince and remarking on his curls and his eyelashes. When he stirred, they took fright and scrambled to hide behind me.

"You're safe here, my lord," I said to assure him. "You've been wounded, but well looked after. Now you must rest and regain your strength."

"I dreamed of wolves," he said, his voice scarce rising above a whisper.

"Yes, Your Highness."

His eyes opened wide. "They were real, then?"

"It is true you saw wolves; but I cannot say they were real, not such as are found in nature. They did much grievous harm, my lord."

A shadow passed over his features then. "Were many killed?"

I hung my head. "The king, your brother," I said.

"My brother?" he snapped as though I were responsible.

"Aye, my lord."

"Dead?"

I nodded.

"You are sure?"

I nodded again. "I was there."

He closed his eyes.

"What about my mother? And my poor sister whose wedding day it was?"

"I don't know, sire. I didn't see. I suppose we could hope . . ."

He snorted and turned aside. I shooed the little girls away and waited to hear what he would say next.

The girls must have run to tell their mother that the prince was awake, for soon she came in and knelt beside me.

"This is Margaret," I said. "She is a wisewoman, well known in these parts for healing gentlefolk as well as common. She tended to your wounds last night and gives you safe hiding here in her house."

Winifred's mother bowed as deeply as she could while kneeling. "Your Majesty," she whispered, "I would touch your cheeks and forehead, if I may. To see if you are feverish."

"All right."

She did it with the back of her hand.

"Am I? Feverish?"

"Somewhat. I would look at the wound now. If I may."

"Go ahead. Do whatever is needed."

She bowed low again, got up, and went to a chest that stood in the corner. Soon she was back with a wooden box filled with small vials and little clay pots. She sent one of the younger girls, who'd been lingering in the doorway, to bring in a bucket of water. Then she began carefully unwrapping the bandages. She needed my help with this. The prince had to be lifted so the bands could be unwound; he was too weak to do it himself.

"Your shirt and doublet we have put away, my lord. I was able to get most of the blood out—but I fear they will never be such as you would want to wear them again."

"I don't care about my shirt and doublet," he said. He looked down at his shoulder, and his face went pale, for indeed it was a dreadful thing to look upon. The flesh was red and swollen, and here and there blood seeped out from between the stitches.

But Margaret did not say a word. She took a clean cloth, and wet it from the bucket, and washed the shoulder well. Then she opened one of the vials, which held some precious fluid as red as blood but perfectly transparent. I did not much care for the smell of it. It reminded me of my father and the cheap liquor he drank at night.

With great care, she poured this potion over the angry wounds. The prince started.

"Does it sting, my lord?"

"No, it was only cold, that's all. It took me by surprise." He closed his eyes, and I saw the muscles tighten in his jaw. Margaret smiled sweetly, for she knew as well as I did that it hurt him plenty. But he was almost a man, practically a knight. He was determined to bear it nobly.

When she was done, she laid a clean cloth over his shoulder and bid me lift him again so she could put the bandages back on.

"Such redness and swelling are to be expected," she said, her voice matter-of-fact. "I've seen it many a time after an animal bite. But you are young and strong. You'll be swinging a sword with that arm ere long. But for now you must rest and let your body heal. I have a potion, if you wish to take it, sire, that will ease your pain and help you sleep."

"What's in it?"

"Wine, poppy syrup, powder of mandrake root. A few other things."

"Well, I shall take it then, and gladly. But first I must have a word with whoever it was that brought me here, for there are things I need to know."

"The young maid who sits here beside you was one. The other was a boy named Tobias. And also my daughter Winifred."

"Who are you?" he asked me.

"I am Molly, my lord."

"And how was it you found me and came to my rescue?"

And so I told him.

When I had finished, he turned to the wall and did not look at me for many minutes so that I wondered whether I ought to leave him alone with his grief. But after a while he turned back to me again.

"I want you to go to the village and find out what you can. I would know for certain if my mother and sister are dead."

"Tobias has already gone on that errand, lord prince. Only, he went to the market town and not the village. Folk come to market from many places, and so chances are better that someone will have news to tell. Also, we feared that in the village—well, Tobias is a stranger, and uncommonly big and tall. People would notice him, and we do not wish to draw attention to this house."

"What do you mean?"

"Well, my lord, we thought—under the circumstances—it might be best if no one knows you are here. And country folk are curious by nature, as they have little of interest to gossip about. If they see a stranger in the village so soon after the tragedy up at the castle, they are likely to remember that Margaret is a wise-woman and—"

"I see," he said. "You fear they will disturb my rest."

"No, sire. I fear greater harm than that."

He looked at me oddly. "I doubt the wolves will hear the gossip and come attack us here."

Oh, how could he fail to understand?

"It might not be wolves next time," I said.

Annoyance crossed his face. "What are you saying?"

I bit my lip, feeling my face flush. "Your Grace, when the wolves came into the hall last night . . ."

"Yes."

"You were not there to see it. You had left to use the privy. But . . . it was not as you might expect with a pack of wild beasts in a room full of people."

"You said the king was killed."

"I did. But, Your Highness, *only* the king was killed, so far as I know. They walked past all those lords and ladies, and the pages, and the village girls who had come there to sing, and the dwarf couple who played the wedding farce. It was as though they only craved royal blood. They knew your brother and went straight for him. And when they had done their grizzly business in the hall, they went up the stairs, past yet more people, leaving them unharmed . . . looking for you."

"What are you saying?"

"You do not understand, truly?"

"We are cursed," he said with a sneer in his voice. "Is that it?"

"Yes, my lord."

"Enough." he said, and lay back and closed his eyes. "Be away with you. Good Margaret, I will take your potion now."

❦ 17 ❧

What Was Said
in the Market Town

WE BEDDED DOWN in the hayloft, as it was not seemly for common folk such as us to share sleeping space with a prince. It mattered not to me. I'd been awake for most of two days and a night and would gladly have lain down anywhere. And I believe I did sleep for an hour or two, enough to take the edge off my weariness.

Then I rose up with a start and looked around to see what had awakened me so suddenly. A noise, most likely, for the place was hardly quiet. From below came the soft breathing of animals, the shuffle of hooves, the occasional bovine sigh. Closer to hand, scattered around me in the loft, were nine human souls, tossing and snoring as people do in their sleep.

Whatever it was, it had left me strangely uneasy. I felt—how can I describe it?—not entirely safe. And so I sat there, still as death, listening to the world beyond the barn: the chirping of crickets, the croaking of frogs, a rise of wind, the distant barking of a dog. Might there also be, among those commonplace sounds, something else? Something more sinister? The furtive footsteps of an assassin?

The more I thought of it, the more uneasy I became. And so at last I gave up on sleep and crept down the ladder from the loft. I looked about for a weapon and found a scythe hanging on the wall. I took it down and carried it with me out into the moonlit night.

I leaned against the great chestnut tree that stood in Margaret's yard. That way, I figured, my silhouette would not be visible to anyone coming up the road.

The tree was enormous. It must have stood there for a hundred years or more. Its trunk was so massive I could not have wrapped my arms halfway around it. I felt anchored, standing beside it, protected somehow. But it had begun to lose its leaves as trees do in the autumn, and they crackled under my feet. I would have to be still so as not to give myself away. I held the scythe ready to swing if need be.

Behind me I heard someone coming out of the

barn. I peered around the trunk and saw that it was Margaret. I must have awakened her when I left the loft, and so she thought to check on Winifred, whose turn it was to keep watch over the prince. I noticed that she did not stop to unlock the door. Nor did she knock for Winifred to draw a bolt and let her in. She just opened the door.

They had not locked it at all, then—with the prince lying wounded inside! Anyone might come along that road and go into the house.

Now, for certain, I heard footsteps. I tightened my hold on the scythe and stood frozen against the tree. But these were not creeping footsteps—plodding was more like it. Perhaps just some villager coming home from—

Then I saw him and my heart leaped. I left my weapon by the tree and ran out to the road, waving.

"Oh, Tobias," I said. "I was worried."

"You are always worried. It was a long way, that's all. Why aren't you asleep?"

"I was too fretful. Did you learn anything at all?"

"Yes. And I stayed late so that I could hear more. New people kept coming into town."

"Come sit over here and tell me. Then I promise to let you rest."

"What is this?"

"My weapon," I said, taking it from him. "I thought I heard someone coming, and I was afraid—"

"I am glad you didn't use that on me."

"Sit."

"I will."

"Now, tell me."

"They are all dead, Molly. The whole family. Everyone save the prince."

"The queen mother and Elinor, too?"

"Yes."

"Oh, that's horrible. Horrible!"

"Aye, it is."

"Was there anybody else?"

"No. Not a one."

"Not even the porter? I mean, how did the wolves get inside—"

"It's past reason, Molly. There were paupers waiting outside the walls for the table scraps from the banquet. There were guards at the gate and the porter outside the doors. Not a one of them was harmed. And how the gate came to open of itself and the doors to the great hall too—it must have been some kind of magic."

"And the wolves?"

"When it was over, they left the castle as gentle as

lambs, and no one's seen fur nor fang of 'em since—
not anywhere."

"Oh," I said, and felt a shiver run through my
body. I wrapped my arms about my knees and held
myself close.

"There was a lot of talk about the prince, Molly.
Some said the wolves had carried him off or devoured
him whole, so now the kingdom has none to rule it.
But later a man came into town—he was valet to one
of the noble guests—and he set those theories cock-a-
hoop. He said they'd found one of the wolves, dead on
the upper landing."

"With the prince's dagger in his belly."

"Yes."

"What do they think it means, then, as Alaric is
nowhere to be found?"

"That he killed the wolves, then escaped down the
river—the water gate was open and the skiff was gone.
Now they're searching for the boat. It has the king's
crest upon it, Molly."

"Oh. I hadn't considered that."

"Nor I."

"We have to hide it, then. Or sink it."

"It's too late. The skiff has been down there all
day. Folk from the village go to the river for water.

With or without the king's crest, a strange boat would be noticed. And by tomorrow they'll have heard about the prince's escape. They know of Margaret's skills with herbs. They'll figure it out, Molly, and come here, sure. They'll have the best intentions but—"

"They'll talk."

"Yes. The whole world shall know of it in a matter of days."

I heard a door shut. Margaret was returning to the barn for a few more hours of rest.

"They don't even lock it," I said.

"Does it matter? The gates of Dethemere Castle couldn't keep those wolves out. What good is a lock on a cottage door?"

We sat a while longer, thinking the same thoughts.

"When?" he asked finally.

"Now. I'm sorry, Tobias. I know you've walked for hours."

"I'll teach you to row."

I laughed. "Can he survive the trip, I wonder?"

"You'll have to call Margaret out again and ask her to give you whatever medicines we might need. And we should dress him like a commoner, leave his fine clothing behind. I'll go down to the boat now and scrape up the paint with a rock, take off the crest if I can."

"Should Winifred come with us?"

"I think it's better if she stays. When people ask about the skiff, she can say it was she who took it, to escape from the castle, and that later it was stolen."

"Yes. That's good."

"Go speak to Margaret now. I'll be back as soon as I can."

He hurried down the path that led to the river. I took up the scythe and headed back to the barn.

Only then did I think to wonder where we were going.

❦ 18 ❧

A Cask
of Herring

MARGARET AND HER HUSBAND, Collum, were not
sorry to see us go. They'd just been scraping by as
it was, without extra mouths to feed and an invalid
to care for night and day. And how it must have
frightened Margaret to hold the future of the kingdom in her hands. What if Alaric should die in her
house?

She provided us with food, and ale, and a blanket to keep the prince warm. She also gave us a little
box with salves, and potions, and bandages in it and
told me what I should do for fever, and for pain, and
should pus appear, and all such things as that. She

had already washed the bloodstains off my gown and Tobias's cotte. Now she gave us Collum's Sunday clothes for the prince to wear.

They were beyond generous, and we could not pay them for any of it.

The prince did give them his golden brooch, as well as his doublet, and hose, and pointy slippers. He must have believed he had thanked them well, as such things were worth a lot of money—even the ruined doublet, for it was embroidered all over with seed pearls and thread of gold. But I knew they were useless to Margaret and her family. A peasant could never sell such finery; people would think it was stolen.

Precious keepsakes—that's all they'd ever be. And knowing how poor the family was, I felt most wretched about it. But Margaret only smiled and bid us Godspeed.

She was a good soul. They all were. Someday, I hoped, the prince would make it up to them.

The moon was just setting when we cast off. Winifred had come down to the river with us and kissed us both good-bye. Then she stood, watching upon the shore, till we were out of sight.

As before, the prince lay curled up on the boards. Only now he was wrapped in Margaret's blanket against the early morning chill. He was quiet for such a long time that I thought he'd fallen asleep. But then I heard his soft voice out of the darkness.

"Where are we going?" he asked.

"First we must be away," Tobias said, "then we will think."

"Can you not think and row at the same time?"

"I shall give it my best effort, Your Majesty."

"I wonder," I said, "if you have formed some thoughts of your own, my lord? Would you like to go to one of your other estates, somewhere at the far reaches of the country, where there are people you trust?"

When he didn't answer right away, I continued.

"For I am not sure that is wise. I think it best not to declare yourself to anyone just yet—till you are healed and know more of what has happened and where the dangers lie."

"You ask me a question, then answer it yourself."

"My apologies, sire. I was not properly raised. I have no manners at all."

"I can see that well enough. But I think in this case you are right."

"I am glad you agree, my lord, for there seems to be a great conspiracy against your family. And now you are the last of the royal line—except for your father's sister, who is old."

"You forget my cousin."

"Him, too. But he and his sons—they are merely a side branch of the family, while you are the tree itself. In truth, I believe you must be the king now, though you have not been crowned. Shall we address you as lord king, Your Majesty?"

"No. I would very much rather you did not."

"As you wish, my lord. But prince or king, you must take great care and not put yourself in danger."

"Then I shall play the peasant for now. I am dressed for it. I suppose I shall have to behave like one too so I may become invisible to those who wish to harm me."

"How is it you think we behave, sire? Common folk, I mean."

"They ask impertinent questions."

"I'm sorry, my lord."

"I know. You have no manners."

"True."

"You still have not given me an answer. Where are we going?"

I had been thinking hard upon this matter and had come up with a plan. Only I didn't like to mention it due to certain drawbacks it would involve. But seeing as no one else had a proposal to make, I sighed and mustered my courage.

"There is an abbey," I said. "Two of my brothers are in service there."

"Your brothers are monks?"

"Oh, my goodness, no. They are only lay servants. Tom works in the stables, and Martin is the almoner's boy."

"I see."

"They will give us food and a bed. It is their duty to care for the poor, out of charity. And they will look after your wounds at the hospice. The monks are said to know much of herbs and healing."

The hospice was one of the drawbacks; I knew the mere thought of it would fill him with disgust. Such places were only for the ragged poor. Gentlemen were nursed by their ladies at home.

But all the prince said was "Hmm."

"My brothers speak well of the abbot. They say he's a good and holy man."

"I would certainly hope so."

"Many are not, my lord."

"What is his name?"

"Elias, I think."

"I don't know him."

"He's a humble sort of abbot. But that seems a good thing, for it means he's not ambitious, nor will he have any great friends."

"And why is that good?"

"Your enemies, my lord—most likely they are in

high places. The abbot will not be connected with folk of that sort, nor will he aim to please them by betraying you."

"Ha! You are more clever than you let on, my girl, and wiser about the world."

"Oh, my lord, I think not."

"I say you are. Stop arguing and just say thank you."

"Thank you, Your Highness."

"So, where is this abbey?" Tobias asked, clearly wishing to change the subject.

"Well, you see," I said, "that's a problem." Here was the other drawback.

He stopped rowing and turned around. "In what way is it a problem?"

"Well . . ."

"*Where is it,* Molly?"

"Oh, all right. It's in the other direction, Tobias. Upstream, against the current. We'd have to pass Winifred's house again and the castle, too, in order to get there."

We were all silent for a long time, each of us thinking hard. I resolved to say no more about it. It was the prince who'd bear the danger and Tobias who'd do the rowing. I'd let them decide.

"Say what you will, my lord, and I will take you there."

Alaric thought some more before he answered. "It seems a likely place to me. But what do you think, Tobias—shall we pull to shore, somewhere remote, and rest till nightfall, then pass those places in the dark?"

"That's exactly what they'll be looking for: a boat pulled ashore in a remote place, downstream from whence it was last seen."

"So what, then?"

"I say we go boldly in the direction none would expect, and by day. I say we turn around and go there now. And—pardon me, my lord—I say we should cover you with the blanket when other boats pass near so that they will think it is only cargo we carry and not a passenger."

"Turn around then and row us back upstream. Now I will have one of those apples and some of that disgusting ale. Then I should like a dose of Margaret's potion that eases the pain and calms the soul. After that you may cover me all you like, and I shall do my best to impersonate a cask of herring."

❧ 19 ❧

Back Up
the River Again

AS WE CAME NEAR Winifred's village again, it started
to rain. The water poured down in great silver sheets,
and though it was cold and unpleasant I thought it a
good omen. People were less likely to go out in such
weather, and those who did kept their heads down.

"We're getting close to the landing now," I said.

"Do you see anyone?" Tobias faced the back of the
boat, as all rowers do, and so he had to turn around to
see what lay ahead.

I squinted. Rainwater was running down from my
hair and into my eyes.

"Yes," I said.

There were two men on the shore, their hoods up against the rain. They were standing exactly where the boat had been tied up, talking and gesturing: *Right there, that's where it was. I'm telling you I saw it yesterday, and the king's crest upon it! A nice little skiff, just like that'n there!*

"Two men," I said. "One just pointed at us."

"Try to act normal," Tobias said. "They can't see us very well in this rain. And the worst they could do now is noise it about the village—and by then we'll be well away."

I leaned over, elbows on knees, chin in my hands. The rain fell on my neck now and ran down into my clothes, which were already soaked through. I glanced over at the men again without turning my head. They continued to stand, arms down now, watching as we disappeared from sight.

It was late afternoon before the clouds parted and we saw blue sky again. Along the banks, water dripped from the trees and sparkled in the sunlight. Flocks of birds swooped over us, searching for food or a place to roost for the night.

I began bailing water out of the boat with cupped hands. It was slow and tedious work and hardly seemed to make a difference. But I kept at it. I didn't think the prince should be lying in the wet like that. He didn't seem to notice, though. In fact, he wasn't moving at all.

"I wonder if Margaret's potion is too strong," I said. "All he does is sleep."

"She said he needed to rest."

"Well, he's doing that, right enough."

"Perhaps it's because of the fever."

I pulled back the soggy blanket and touched his cheek.

"No, Tobias, it's not the fever. He's as cold as death. See how pale he is."

He leaned forward and stared.

"Aye, you're right. He doesn't look well at all."

"What shall we do?"

"Lift him up; see if you can wake him."

I did this, and he moaned once or twice; but still he slept on.

"He's like a poppet," I said. "All flopsy."

"Just hold him, then, as you are. Wrap your arms around him and turn his face to the sun. Lay your cheek against his."

"But what if he should wake?"

"Then that will be good, and we can bid him move around as much as he can to warm himself."

"Oh, don't be such a dimwit," I said. "What if he should wake and find me *draped all over him* in such a familiar manner?"

"I never knew you were a proper lady. Better to let him die, then."

"Oh, you are a warty toad," I said.

In time the warmth of the sun and the warmth of my body seemed to have done him some good. His cheeks now had a bit of color, and he moved about more, moaning and mumbling. Yet still he did not wake.

"Molly?"

"What?"

"How far up the river to your town, and the abbey?"

"I only made the journey once, when I was seven and came to the castle. It took us two days. But I can't say how long it would take going there by boat. The road is straight whereas the river twists and winds."

Tobias nodded. "Will you recognize the place from the water?"

"I think so. I'm sure you can see the church tower from the river."

"Good."

The prince was moving more now, adjusting his position in small ways from time to time. He was coming out of his long sleep. I freed myself from my strange embrace and laid him on the floorboards again.

"He's better now," I whispered. "His heart beats more strongly, and his cheeks are flushed."

"No wonder." He grinned. "So would mine be if you held me like that. I shall be sure to tell the prince what a noble service you did him. Perhaps he will award you a medal."

"You are a spotted slug," I said.

Tobias pulled steadily against the current. He was exhausted, I could tell, yet our pace had varied little all day. Now the sun was near to setting, the sky ablaze with bawdy color.

"It's beautiful," I said.

"Aye. And it betokens good weather, too. Or so the boatmen say."

"I hope they're right."

"We just passed Lord Hargrove's estate, Molly. We'll come to the castle soon."

"I wonder how it'll look."

"Much as before, I'd expect."

"But I mean—what if everybody fled, as we did, and all is just as it was: bodies lying on the floor and dishes upon the table, all swarming with ants and rats, and no other living soul in that great empty castle but the wandering ghosts of dead kings."

"Heaven help us, Molly! What a horrible thought."

"I know. It just keeps popping into my head."

"Like the visions you saw in the silver bowl?"

"Hush," I said.

"He can't hear us."

"No, Tobias, it's not the same, not in the slightest. For my visions are real and true. These are just . . . foolish imaginings."

He didn't speak for a while. Then, "I wish your voices were guiding us now."

"You might not like it if they did."

"Perhaps not, but if danger lies ahead, I'd be glad to know it in advance."

"Well, I can no more bid my visions come than I can make them go away. Oh, look, Tobias. There's the castle tower."

"See if you can wake the prince."

"My lord?" I whispered, shaking him gently. "We are close on to the castle now. I must cover you again; you must lie as still as a stone and be absolutely quiet."

He grunted something I took for assent but went on squirming.

"Lord prince," I hissed, "you must not move! We are passing the castle now."

Tobias was picking up speed—not by rowing faster, but by putting more power into each stroke. He kept his head down most of the time, only turning now and again to see that he was steady on his course. It was a fine performance. Anyone would think him just a common boatman, tired and soaked from a wet day on the river, anxious to get home to his fire.

"The castle's all lit up," I said. "So many torches."

"Shhh," Tobias said.

We had come to the bridge that spanned the river between the guardhouse and the castle. There were mounted knights up there, just outside the gate. That was unusual. Who were they guarding, and from what?

I leaned over the prince, shielding him from view and hiding my face. My hand rested on our "cargo"—the prince's arm—and I pressed firmly in warning.

It grew dark as we slipped under the bridge, and the splash of the oars echoed eerily against the stone. I could hear the sound of horses' hooves overhead.

"Shhh," Tobias said again, very quietly.

We came out at last into the faint evening light, and I drew a deep breath of relief, for I have never liked dark, close places. I heard a man overhead shout, "Hey!" The bridge was behind us now, and I didn't want to turn around and look.

"It's all right," Tobias said, his voice soft. "Nothing to do with us. One knight calling to another, most like."

Stroke, stroke, stroke. I thought we'd never reach

the point where the river bends, hugging the castle on two sides. From there we would no longer be able to see the bridge—nor could the soldiers see us.

When first I'd arrived in service, I thought the river had put itself there to be nearer to the king. I smiled, thinking of that now. Of course the bend in the river had been there first, long before someone came along and thought: What a perfect place to build a castle! The river would act as a ready-made moat, protecting it from invaders on two sides. And it would be so handy for emptying latrines and chamber pots, and disposing of dead rats, and garbage, and dirty dishwater.

And you could also put a water gate on the river, convenient for coming and going, for loading and unloading goods—and escaping from demonic wolves.

We were almost there now, and I felt the grip of fear as the iron grate came into sight. Would there be a new boat tied up at the landing? Would someone be in it, watching, ready to glide out after us as we passed?

But the grate was shut tight; and if there was a new boat, I didn't see it.

On we went, till it was full dark, and still Tobias rowed upstream. It seemed hours had passed since we'd passed a village and heard the tolling of a curfew bell, alerting the good folk of the town to bank their fires, and cover them, and put out their candles for the night. Except for the gentle sound of the oars and the occasional barking of a dog, it was dead quiet.

A three-quarters moon was rising by then, glowing dimly through a bank of clouds low on the horizon. Above us were countless twinkling stars. I marveled at them, and wondered how they got there, and what it would be like to touch one, and where they went in the daytime.

And for that brief moment, at least, the world seemed a good place, mysterious and full of promise.

❦ 20 ❧

Who Am I
to Be?

TOBIAS FOUND A LIKELY PLACE to pull over for the
night. It was a small inlet, sheltered by a strip of
bushes that grew along the edge of the river. The
bank had a gentle slope, perfect for landing a skiff.
And not far inland was a grassy clearing surrounded
by tall trees.

The prince was wide-awake by then, having slept
the better part of two days. While we emptied our sup-
plies out of the boat and tipped it over to let out the
standing water, Alaric found himself a rock to sit upon
and wrapped himself well in our only blanket.

"How far is it from here to the abbey?" he asked

when we came into the clearing. "Can we get there by tomorrow?"

"I can't say for sure," I said. "I've never gone there by boat, only walked; and that took two days."

"I think," Tobias said, "if we continue by water, we will have to sleep rough another night, as the river has many curves and bends, and we are going upstream. But if we leave at first light and cut across to join the road, we might reach the abbey before vespers tomorrow. It's more direct—though I fear, my lord, you are not up to walking so far."

"I may be weak from my wound, but I am otherwise strong. And I have learned to bear what I must."

"Is that your wish, then? To abandon the boat and walk the rest of the way?"

"Yes," he said. "Now give me something to eat or I shall waste away to nothing but bones and flesh."

Tobias cut a thick slice of bread, set a hunk of Margaret's cheese upon it, and handed it to the prince. Alaric took a bite, then grunted and spat into the bushes. "The saints protect me!" he cried. "This bread is wet!"

"It rained, my lord," Tobias said.

"And the cheese is revolting."

"I'm afraid it was all that Margaret had to offer us."

"So is this what you people eat? Can you possibly

like it?" He asked this as though it were a real question.

"It drives the hunger away, my lord."

The prince gazed long at Tobias, who sat quietly upon the ground, the loaf in one hand, a knife in the other, his expression remarkably calm.

"So it does," Alaric said. "So it does. Now, I believe I shall have a cup of that exceptional ale, if you please, to wash down this delicious cheese."

I turned my head so he wouldn't see me smile.

When we'd finished our meal and packed everything away, we set to planning for the day ahead, working out what stories we would tell the monks when we arrived at the abbey.

Tobias and I had no need to dissemble. We had only to tell the truth: that we were servants who had fled the castle after the tragedy of the wedding feast. We'd decided to go to St. Bartholomew's since my brothers were in service there. And as our master the king was now dead and we had no money or support of any kind, we hoped the good monks would take us in and give us work to do.

The prince, though—he was a problem.

"I don't think I can pass for a commoner," he said. "They would see through me in a moment, as I neither look nor speak like one. What if we say I was a guest at the wedding, and was wounded by one of the wolves, and fled?"

I had been afraid it would come to this. "Why then, my lord, are you dressed in Collum's Sunday clothes?"

"Because . . . mine were torn and stained with blood. I fled the castle and went to a nearby village, where I was treated by a leech. I bought these clothes from him, as there was nothing of quality to be had in such a place."

"But, sire," I went on, "would you not be too injured to walk that far?"

"I suppose—"

"Did someone help you, or were you alone? What was the name of the village and who was the leech?"

"I don't know. I don't know!"

I held my tongue for a little while. He was clever enough. He'd see how it was if he tried.

"I shall say I am a stranger to this country, arrived only recently for the wedding. And so, of course, I don't know the region well. And besides, I was insensible with pain and can recall very little of that night."

I said nothing. Neither did Tobias.

"So? What do you think?"

I took a deep breath and let it out. "My lord," I said. "I think it's a terrible idea."

He recoiled.

"Oh?" he said. "And why is it so terrible?"

"Well, first of all it is widely known, and much talked of, that only members of the royal family died that day. The creatures harmed no one else. So if you go to the abbey and present yourself as a gentleman who'd been at the wedding feast and was bit by a wolf, won't it set them to wondering: *Isn't Prince Alaric missing?*"

"I see."

"That's not all. We hope to stay at the abbey a month or more, until you are well healed. During that time, other visitors will come and go, often staying for only one night. Say, eight one day, ten the next, six more the day after. If you go to the abbey as a gentleman, they will seat you at table with the other highborn folk. What chance is there, among so many, that there will not be at least one who will recognize you?"

"I have lived away from my country since I was a child."

"But you were at the wedding, my lord. All the guests saw you, full grown, marching into the hall, sitting up there at the high table. What chance is there, I ask you again, that not a single one of those guests should pass through Riverton on some errand or other and need a bed for the night?"

It grew very quiet, then. The prince leaned forward, his hands clasped, arms between his long legs—thinking.

"Very little chance at all," he finally said.

Had Alaric slapped me for my ill manners or spit curses upon me, I wouldn't have been surprised. But to *agree* with me—that was most unexpected.

"Lord prince," I said as gently as I knew how, "you are safer among the poor."

"Yes, I see that is so. Tell me then, clever Molly, what it is you propose?"

"You will not like it, sire."

"Oh, I have no doubt about that whatsoever. But I shall hear it all the same."

"I agree that you should say you are foreign. That idea was very good, for I did fear the way you talk would likely give you away."

"But if he is foreign," Tobias said, "he must speak a different language, or at least in some strange and particular way."

"I can do that," Alaric said. "I've lived many years in Austlind and am fluent in their dialect."

"Then let us say you are a merchant from the border region between here and Austlind. Can you come up with a town you know of? Someplace small?"

"I can."

"Good. So, you often come over the border to Westria to sell your wares—pots, wool, sommat like that. Only, you have a weakness for ale and so you stopped at a tavern, and stayed there too long, and got roaringly drunk."

I heard Tobias draw breath. He was sure I had gone too far.

"And as you were ruined for drink, a pair of thieves stole your horse and wagon, and your money, and all the wares you had not yet sold. Then they knocked you into a ditch and set their dog upon you. It must be an animal bite, my lord. The monks will know what it is the minute they take the bandages off."

I waited. In the darkness, I heard him making strange sounds, and I thought for a moment he was choking. Also, he was moving strangely, bending backward and forward. Then he burst into a raucous laugh.

"The saints' eyelids! Who has raised this devil child? Is there more? Please tell me I am not a cut-purse as well as a drunk."

I let him take the time, laugh himself out—for I had one more thing to ask of him, and I knew it would be hard.

"Sire," I said when the time seemed right, "would you mind most terribly if we cut off your hair?"

❦ 21 ❧

The Abbey

TOBIAS BASHED THE FLOOR of the boat with a rock. Then well before sunrise the following morning we set it loose into the current. It would begin to fill with water, a little at a time, until it finally sank at some place far downstream. Then we awakened the prince, and broke our fast, and headed off through the trees in the direction of the road.

It was a long walk for someone in pain, and the prince said little along the way. Now and then he would stop, gasping, and say he must sit down. And so we would rest, but never for long.

By midafternoon it became clear that unless we picked up our pace we would not reach the abbey in time to be admitted there. The gates would be shut for the night. Alaric did his best to walk faster, clinging tightly to Tobias's arm, leaning forward, taking long strides. But he was pale and sweating and looked horribly ill. At one point he staggered away from us and vomited into the bushes.

"Tobias," I whispered, "he can't do it. I think we should stop now, sleep another night in the woods. He'll be fresh in the morning, and we won't have so far to go."

"No," Tobias said. "A wound can go bad in a day, and I didn't much like how it looked this morning. He needs expert care, and we cannot give it to him."

The prince was back now, wiping his mouth with his sleeve.

"Here, my lord," I said. "Why don't you lean on me for a while? I'm smaller than Tobias, just low enough to be comfortable."

Wordlessly, he laid his good arm across my shoulders; I held him firmly around the waist, and we continued down the road.

I am embracing a prince, I thought. *And this time he is awake.*

I was so close I could smell him—the common sweat-stink of his borrowed clothes, and beneath that some costly perfume with just a hint of soap. He must have bathed before dressing for the banquet, and the scent still lingered. I felt myself blushing and turned away.

The sun was low in the sky when we began to pass through the abbey lands. The fields were empty now, bare of all but stubble, the harvest already in. We passed the mill, and the beehouse, and the fish pond, and the bakehouse, and the brewery. But we saw no monks about. They were already back within the walls, then, at supper most likely.

We rounded a bend, and the abbey gate came into view. Tobias groaned. "Too late," he said. "And after so much effort."

"No, wait," I said. "Over there." I pointed to where a crowd was gathered by another, smaller door. They seemed to be mostly poor widows, together with their raggedy children; but there were others, too, who just looked old, or feeble, or sick. One man conversed with invisible air, gaping, and grinning, and waving his arms.

The poor always waited for alms outside the houses of the great. So, too, at the abbey. Every evening when the monks had finished their supper, the almoner would gather up the scraps and take them out to the paupers. On occasion he might have a few coins for them, too, or a bit of candle wax, or some old clothes.

We took our places at the edge of the crowd and waited.

"Remember," I whispered to Alaric, "you are Sebastian the foreign merchant now."

He said "Ya," or sommat like that, in a foreign-sounding way. Then grabbing my arm for balance, he lowered himself to the ground and sat leaning against the wall. He breathed heavily, his eyes closed.

Before long the door swung open. The paupers brought out their little cups and bowls and formed a proper line. There was no pushing or shouting; they knew there would be plenty for all.

The almoner carried a basket of bread, fresh from the abbey bakehouse. Each loaf was split in two, as the ration was half a loaf per person. In his other hand he held the almadish, filled with broken bits of fish, some carrots and turnips, and the remnants of the monks' hard-bread trenchers, now soaked in sauce from the meal.

Behind the almoner came his assistant, a fine-looking lad with clear skin and bright, dark eyes. He was dressed like a monk in a homespun robe, but he was not in holy orders. He wasn't even a novice, just a humble, illiterate lay brother, a servant of the abbey. He carried a tankard of ale, and as the paupers passed by, he poured some into each of their cups.

I had not seen him for years, but I'd have known that face anywhere.

I stepped forward. The almoner handed me a half-loaf. I curtsied to him in thanks, then quickly turned to the lad, who noted that I had no cup for the ale and seemed uncertain what to do.

"Martin?" I said.

He stared at me, eyes squinting.

"Martin Stinky-Toes-Frog-Face?"

"*Molly*?" he said. "Can that be you?"

"None other!"

"Oh, my stars! Brother!" he said to the almoner. "This here is my sister." Then, still gaping in wonder, he set down the tankard and hugged me hard. "Oh, Molls, how I feared for you when I heard what happened at the castle."

"I know. It was horrible."

"Did you see—?"

"Yes." I cut him off, not wishing the prince to hear such painful talk. "Then we ran away—me and my friend Tobias. We hoped to find shelter here, and work too. We'd like to stay on, as we have nowhere else to go."

"Come in," the almoner said, turning toward the

door. "We'll find you beds for the night and talk about work on the morrow. I must hurry now or I shall be late for night prayers."

The paupers were already drifting away. Having been fed, they would move off into the town, to whatever humble shelter they could find for the night. One of the widows looked back at us. *They are the lucky ones,* she must have been thinking. *They'll sleep in a bed tonight.*

"Excuse me, brother almoner," I said, "but there is someone else with us." I pointed to where Alaric sat, still leaning against the wall. "We met him on the road. He came here from Austlind and was robbed and beaten; then a dog was set upon him. Now he's penniless and alone and sorely wounded. Do you think he might—?"

"Of course," the almoner said. "Help the man up, Martin. Let us go inside."

As I watched Prince Alaric shuffle through the door, clinging to my brother's arm, I marveled at how he'd changed in only a matter of days. Dirty and sunburned now, with stubble upon his cheeks and ragged, knife-cut hair, his humble clothes rumpled and stained with mud—he was the very image of a common man who had tumbled into misfortune.

His mother, may she rest in peace, wouldn't have known him.

When the almoner had locked the door, he called to a passing novice. "You, there, Brother Robert. Come and take this poor fellow to the hospice."

"But I shall be late for Compline," the boy said.

"God will forgive you this once. And when you get him there and settled in a bed, I want you to wait till Brother Eutropious returns. Tell him this man was dog-bit and his wound needs looking to. Understand?"

The boy nodded.

"Then go. Can you not see he is about to drop?"

"Yes, brother."

"Your friend will be in excellent hands," said the almoner as we watched the prince walk slowly away. "Now see to your sister, Martin, and to young Tobias, too. I must go to prayer."

⤙ ⤚

We ate our half-loaves and what remained of the paupers' scraps, washing it all down with several cups of ale—and very good ale it was, too, from the monks' own brewery. While we ate, Martin ran upstairs to the dormitory where the lay brothers slept. Soon he came scampering back down again accompanied by a gangly lad with honey-brown eyes. His sandy hair was cut close to the head, so his ears were even more prominent than they usually were: my brother Tom.

"Spider-Legs-Elephant-Ears!" I crowed.

"Will you look at that!" He took me in his arms and squeezed me half to death. "Wicked Little Molls, all growed up!"

"They fed us at the castle," I said.

"And you didn't miss a meal."

"Not a one."

Then the smile slid off his face. "You heard about Ma?"

"Yes," I said. "Do you go back there much?" I didn't say *home.*

"Once a year, Molls. At Christmas, same as always."

"Does Tucker still work in the cutting room?"

"He does all the tailoring now. Pa's taken to drink."

"Taken?"

"Well, it's worse now."

"And Anne? Is she married, or still keeping house for Pa?"

"Keeping house," Martin said. "She did find herself a sweetheart, only Father wouldn't give her a dowry. Not a farthing, Molls. So the fellow went and married someone else." He kicked the ground with his boot. "Father shoulda died, not Ma."

Tom shrugged. "The devil wouldn't take him, I guess."

Tobias cleared his throat, then. I think he was embarrassed.

"Sorry," Martin said. "Family talk. Forgot you were there."

"That's all right. I'm very forgettable."

"You are not!" I said. "You just have better manners than we do. This is my friend Tobias, Tom. He worked up at the castle too. In the stables, same as you."

"Chaw! Really?"

"Yes," Tobias said. "Carting mostly, and other odd work. Hauling."

"You thinking to stay on here, then, along with Molls? I could talk to the constable about you tomorrow. We've been a lad short since September when old Gustav was taken up for stealing."

"I'd like that," Tobias said. "Thanks."

"Mind you, there's not much goes on around here—mostly praying, and lots of work."

"That's fine with me."

"All right," Martin said. "Then we'd best get you settled. Compline will soon be over, and we're all supposed to be quiet. Tom, take Tobias upstairs and find him a pallet. I'll go with Molls to see the matron."

"G'night then," Tom whispered. "Wicked Little Molls!"

I took Martin's arm, and we crossed the yard in the growing darkness. "Was I really as bad as all that?"

"No. You were never wicked, only wild. You'd say most anything, whatever you heard on the streets."

"Still do," I said. "Stinky-Toes-Frog-Face." I gave his arm a squeeze. "Now, tell me about the matron."

"Well, she's a great, plump widow with a ruddy face, and a large nose, and the best heart in the world. She looks after the women who visit here, commoners and highborn ladies alike. She'll look after you as well."

"Will she give me work?"

"I expect so."

I leaned my head on Martin's shoulder, feeling safe and protected.

I decided on the spot that I would stay there forever. I'd work for the good-hearted matron, and see my brothers and Tobias every day—for in my fantasy, he would stay there forever too. He'd go over to the hospice in the mornings and visit Sebastian the merchant (I couldn't go, of course, because I was a girl); then in the afternoons he'd tell me all about it, and the news would always be good.

Then one day Sebastian would walk out of the

hospice, whole and strong, his cheeks pink and his beautiful curls all grown back, ready to declare himself to the world and take his rightful place on the throne of Westria. But first he'd thank us heartily for everything we'd done. He'd kiss me on the cheeks, and say what a wonder I was, how I'd saved his life, and stood by him in time of need, and all such things as that. I'd weep when he left and feel an aching in my heart. But as long as I lived, whenever King Alaric was spoken of, I'd remember that he was *my* Alaric, and we had shared our special moments together, and I had held him in my arms. . . .

I know how that sounds—like a foolish, sentimental fairy tale, especially the part about the prince. But oddly enough, it wasn't far off the mark. That's how things actually happened, at least for a while.

I did find work in the women's quarters, sweeping floors, and serving at meals, and helping with the linens on wash days. The matron was much in need of my help, as there were rather more noble visitors at the abbey than was common. Indeed, every one of the private rooms was occupied.

I recognized some of the ladies as guests from the wedding and thought what a blessing it was that Alaric had listened to me. For if he'd come to the abbey as he'd wished, in the character of a nobleman, he would have been found out for sure. Instead he was hidden away, safe and anonymous, in the sick ward with the paupers, growing stronger every day.

It was a season of healing for me as well.

I'd never known what family meant. There was an empty place in my heart where that knowledge should have been. For though I had many brothers and sisters, they were mostly gone before I was old enough to know them; and those who remained had not the time to spare for me. My mother dwelt in a world of her own, and the less said about Father, the better. I don't think I'd have been such a wild little thing if I'd had someone warm to come home to.

Now, for the first time, I did. For Matron took me to her heart like the child she'd never had; Tobias was nearby, just across the way in the stable yard; and my brothers were forever popping up—calling me Wicked Little Molls and squeezing the breath out of me whenever they took the fancy. It was like having a real family, and it softened me. When the world around you is orderly and calm, and you are spoken to with kindness, and praised, and petted, and teased—why, there's no need to be wary and ready with your fists.

You know how people say there's always a lull

before the storm? It's true. Those quiet months when I felt so at peace—that was the lull. And it was well that I enjoyed it, for when the winds came, they rose suddenly. And soon I would be out in that storm, in the very center of that storm, with no protection in sight.

❦ 22 ❧

The Storm

COMPLINE, OR NIGHT PRAYERS, marked the end of the day. After that, the Great Silence began. We were not supposed to utter a word until breakfast the following morning.

But I didn't like to go to bed with the sun; nor was I much inclined to silent reflection. And so most nights if the weather was fair I'd go outside and sit on the dormitory steps. I rarely went alone. There was usually someone with a story to tell, and the time to sit there and tell it. We kept our voices low. Nobody heard us.

On that particular evening I was with my bedmate, Alice. She'd been at the abbey for a couple of weeks, looking for work in the town. She was a good talker and had entertained me with many tales of her adventures. But I'd wondered how it happened that she was cut adrift as she was, traveling the roads alone. And so, on that occasion, I asked.

"My parents made a match for me," she said, "and I wouldn't agree to it. So they disowned me and turned me out."

"But why did you refuse him? Was he old and ugly?"

"Middling old," she said. "And middling ugly. But that was not the reason."

"What was it then?"

"The last wife he had, he beat her to death."

"No!"

"Yes."

"But why would your father choose such a man?"

"He was big in the town. A cloth merchant. He's middling rich, too. Father thought him a catch."

"Ah," I said. "So how have you managed since without a penny to your name?"

"Who said I had not a penny?"

"You said they disowned you. I just thought . . . did they give you some money, then, before they sent you away?"

"Of course not."

"Well?"

"I took it, Molly." She laughed at my astonishment. "Father thought I didn't know where they kept the money, but I did. I only took my dowry. They'd been glad enough to pay it and be rid of me." She shrugged. "So they did pay it, and they are rid of me."

"You can't go back then. Not ever."

"No. Not that I would want—"

"What is that?" I asked, sniffing the air.

"The bakehouse, most likely."

"No. Not at night. And the bakehouse is too far away to smell so strong. And this is not sweet and yeasty like—"

A novice came running past us, then, skirts flying, sandals slapping against the flagstones.

"Fire!" he yelled. "Awake! Awake!"

"Where?" Alice called after him, jumping to her feet. But he did not answer, just kept calling the alarm: "Awake! Awake!"

Moments later the church bell started ringing, loud and insistent: *Clang! Clang! Clang!* Doors opened and the inhabitants of the abbey came straggling into the yard, fastening their clothes, running fingers through tousled hair, looking about them to see where they ought to go.

"This way!" a monk called, and the crowd followed.

Still, I sat unmoving, except that I was trembling violently—for, heaven help me, the voice in my head had come again: *"I'm sorry!"* it cried. *"They're too much for me now. Please, you must help—"*

"Come on!" Alice said, grabbing my hand and pulling me up. "They'll need many hands to haul the water."

I shook myself like a wet dog. *Go away,* I told the voice. *Leave me alone.*

We raced down the stairs and melted into the crowd. The air was bitter with smoke, but there was no sign of flames till we rounded the corner by the south gate. And then I saw it: the hospice was burning.

The monks were still bringing buckets from wherever they were kept, handing them out, then hurrying back for more. I wormed my way to the front of the crowd, and what I saw—oh, it made the roots of my hair rise up and my skin go all to prickles.

How could it have gotten that bad so quickly, before anyone raised the alarm, before anyone smelled smoke?

No one could possibly have survived it.

Already a line was forming between the well and the roaring fire, people passing water-filled buckets from one hand to the next, then passing the empty ones back to be refilled. I spotted Martin among them.

He waved me over, and I joined the brigade. There was no hope of saving the hospice; that was obvious to all of us. But we might at least keep the flames from spreading.

It was heavy work and my arms ached, but I was grateful for it. Had I not been given a task to do, I think mad rage would have consumed me as surely as the fire was consuming the hospice.

Not long after, we heard a crash, and the air filled with fiery sparks. The roof had collapsed. But we still went on passing buckets for an hour, maybe more—until at last the word came down the line that the fire had been put out. It was safe to go in and search for bodies.

Four stretchers were already laid out in the court-yard by the time I got there, each containing a body covered with a sooty shroud. I saw Tobias kneeling beside one of them. He'd pulled the sheet back and was studying the face. Then he covered the corpse again and went to the next one. Then the next. Not Alaric, then. Not yet.

I heard shouts: another body had been found. I didn't want to look—indeed I dreaded it more than words can tell—but I went back to the hospice all the same.

Four or five monks were there, wading through

the smoky ruins. They wore heavy boots and leather gloves, and their robes were hiked up above their knees, held in place with cords of rope. They were leaning over, hauling charred timbers out of the way.

I watched as they lifted the body out—nothing now but a great, black lump that had formerly been a man. I thought I would be sick, but I couldn't stop watching to vomit. They set the remains on a waiting stretcher. Now there were five.

Tobias studied that one too, as soon as it was set down by the others. Then he got to his feet and looked toward the hospice to see if they were bringing out more bodies. Instead he spotted me. He came over then and wrapped me in his arms.

"Oh, Molly," he said.

"He might have escaped, Tobias. There's a chance. Weren't there more than five men being cared for in that place?"

"Oh, ten at least. Maybe fifteen."

"Even at his worst he walked all that way to get here, and he's had near two months to mend. Surely he could run out a door."

"Of course he could."

"Then let's go find him."

Tobias went one way and I another, moving through the crowd, searching for that one familiar face. I didn't know which monks had worked among the sick, so I stopped each one I passed and asked about Sebastian. But they all said the same thing: they'd recovered five bodies; beyond that they knew nothing.

Finally, I asked the right person. Yes, he said, there were survivors. They'd been taken to the garden behind the Lady Chapel.

"Oh, bless you, brother," I said, grabbing his hand and nearly crushing it with joy. Then I left him staring in astonishment as I ran away.

A cluster of people were gathered in the garden. Some were sitting on the ground, a few on stone benches. A handful of brothers were looking after them.

The moon hadn't risen yet, so it was dark in the garden. I couldn't make out their faces from where I stood, not in the dim light. So I went in close, going from man to man, carefully studying each one. They were all smeared with soot, and many were sick from the smoke; but only one was seriously burned. The monks had already loaded him onto a stretcher.

It was dreadful to hear his cries. I'd burned my hand a time or two and well remembered the pain. But this man was raw and blistered all over; his clothes had burned right off of him. Oh, how that poor man suffered—it must have been beyond bearing. The rage in my heart rose up again.

I turned away. I couldn't watch anymore.

And that was when I saw them: an old man wearing nothing but a blackened shirt, sitting on the dead grass, wheezing and coughing and trembling with the cold, his pale, bony legs stretched out before him. And there beside him, offering him a cup of water—was Alaric.

❦ 23 ❧

The Messenger

IN THE EARLY MORNING it started to rain. I lay awake listening to the rattling on the roof and the quiet snores of the women around me. Tired though I was, I couldn't sleep for thinking about the fire, and those shrouded corpses, and the burned man—and other things.

The prince had escaped death once again, but it didn't mean he was safe. Hiding him had clearly done no good; the curses had followed him to the abbey—for I had no doubt those flames were demon-sent. It was unnatural how they had risen up so fast and burned so hot. And that the fire should target the hospice in particular—it was far too personal, too particular, like wolves that only craved royal blood. And they would keep coming after him, again and again, however many times as it took. . . .

I got up, and dressed, and went outside.

It had turned windy and bitter cold; the rain would turn to snow soon. I pulled up the hood of my cape, and walked down the stairway to a covered walkway, and sat there on one of the benches. It calmed me to be out in the chill air watching the gray dawn.

After a while the bell rang for Prime. The monks would be making their way down the night stairs and into the church to pray. In the dormitories, departing guests would start gathering their belongings, cursing the rain, thinking how muddy the roads were going to be.

I got up and headed to the kitchen to help with breakfast.

It was then that I noticed the messenger. He'd just dismounted and handed the reins to a stable lad. Now he strode across the great court in the direction of the abbot's chamber, a roll of paper in a waterproof case clutched firmly in his hand.

He was in there for about an hour—a fact that everyone in the abbey seemed to know. Either he had a very long message to deliver or, more likely, he stopped to have sommat to eat. Whichever it was, he left the abbot's quarters just as briskly as he'd gone in. He collected his mount and rode out again, off to other towns and villages, spreading his message throughout the region.

We had just finished cleaning up from breakfast when the bell started ringing in the tower. As it was early yet for the monks' next service, we were clearly being called to hear the news.

Inside and out of the abbey walls, brothers and servants left off work. Novices put away their books. Visitors who had just set out turned back. It would not surprise me if some townsfolk came too, such was the crowd in the church.

It was the custom for the monks and the novices to stand up front, the rest of us behind. So even when I rose up on my toes, there was nothing before me but a sea of tonsured heads, each with its own shiny bald spot circled by a fringe of hair. It has never been explained to me why monks shave their heads in this particular way. Maybe they wish to look old and wise.

There was a rustling in the crowd, and I looked up at the pulpit; I thought it likely that the abbot would address us from there. And sure enough, here came his head, followed by his shoulders, and then the rest of him. He reached the top and stood for a moment, hands folded on the lectern, gazing down at us and waiting for silence. Finally, he began.

He spoke of the fire, and of those who'd died—six in all: five of the sick and the man I'd seen who was so badly burned. He'd been a novice, just fourteen. The abbot said some prayers in Latin, which I didn't understand. Then he read out the names of the dead and told us a few things about each of them.

That part I liked.

They knew the novice well, of course. The abbey had been his home since he was just a little child. He'd grown up there and was soon to have been ordained a deacon.

The other five, though, had been strangers. They'd come out of nowhere, desperately poor and desperately sick; and their histories were all much the same. Still, the abbot did his best. Whatever small bits of information each man had given to the porter when he arrived, or later to the monks who treated him, or to another patient in the next bed over—the place where he had lived, perhaps, or the wife who'd died, or the farm that had failed—the abbot told us those things.

I wept. Most everybody did.

"The funeral mass will be in two days," the abbot said when he had finished. "God rest their souls. Let us rejoice that so many were spared."

He paused for a moment and took a deep breath. He wasn't finished yet.

"There is another reason I have called you here. As you may already know, we were visited by a messenger this morning. He brought important news regarding the royal succession." He cleared his throat. "As our king and all his heirs have perished"—there were gasps all around—"the crown of Westria shall go to King Reynard of Austlind, as he is the son of Gertrude, sister to our late king Godfrey."

"But the prince!" someone shouted from the crowd. Others picked up the cry.

"What about Alaric?"

"Do they know for sure he is dead?"

The abbot raised his hand and waited till we grew quiet again.

"It is believed," he said, "that the prince was drowned."

"But the body!" people cried. "Did they find his body?"

"No," Elias said. "They have not found him, only the wreckage of the skiff in which he escaped. But it was the king's boat. That is certain, for it bore the royal crest."

I was so startled that I stepped back, nearly crushing the toes of a woman behind me. "Oh, I'm sorry!"

I said, touching her arm. But she only waved me away. Her eyes remained fixed on the abbot as she blotted tears from her cheeks with the corner of her apron.

So they'd found our ruined boat, with no sign of the prince anywhere. It'd be a natural assumption that the prince had drowned. But then they'd gone and added the bit about the royal crest—and that had given them away. Because it wasn't there; I knew it for a fact. Tobias had scraped it off.

It was a lie, then, not an honest mistake. Reynard had no body to show to the people and rightfully claim the throne, so he'd embroidered himself a tale, added that one little detail to make it more believable: it wasn't just *any* boat they'd found washed up on some mudbank, or half sunk in shallow water—no, it was the *king's* boat, the very same one that was missing from the water gate!

I felt my hands ball into fists.

"My children!" the abbot boomed over the sounds of whispers and weeping. "Please hear me out to the end. We will never get through this if you will not listen."

The crowd was abashed. There were little gasps and sniffles as they tried to control themselves. Finally it grew quiet and the abbot went on.

"There is a document," he said, "that bears the late

King Mortimer's seal, and supports Reynard's claim. It states that in the absence of a living male descendant, the succession then goes through the female line— that is to say, through his daughter Gertrude to her son, Reynard. This is in accord with ancient custom.

"And so it appears that he shall be our new king. And as he also rules Austlind, our countries shall be joined. I fear we will lose our name—become part of Austlind, or West Austlind, perhaps."

He waited for the burst of outrage that did not come. The outrage was there, all right; but he'd implored us to hold our tongues and hear him out, and this we were determined to do. The abbot blinked, cleared his throat, and continued.

"As Reynard was already in the country, having come to Westria for the wedding, he has stayed on at Dethemere Castle. To be more precise, he has taken possession of it and has sent for knights from Austlind to man it properly. He wishes to assure us we have nothing to fear." I heard scorn in his voice as he said this. "He will see that no factions rise up and cause a disturbance among us as happened after Mortimer died. He will see that the transition is peaceful and orderly."

Elias bowed his head. Then, "That is all." His

voice came deep out of his chest, full of emotion. I thought he was close to tears. "May God sustain us in these terrible times." Then he crossed himself and, clinging tightly to the rail as he went, slowly descended the circular stairs that led down from the pulpit and disappeared from sight.

The crowd began to disperse, people wiping their faces, muttering to one another, heads hung in sorrow. But I did not move. I would stay there awhile, till everyone had gone and I was alone in that cavernous space, where the stained-glass windows glowed in the pale morning light and, in the chapels along both sides of the nave, candles twinkled before holy images. I thought I might work things out more easily in such a place as that. Perhaps God might even notice me and offer a word of advice. He never had before, but perhaps he would take an interest now, as it concerned great matters this time, not just me and my little unimportant problems.

I craned my neck and looked up at the highest part of the ceiling, where the columns curved and became arches, then met at a point in the middle. I wondered if God sat up there looking down at us.

Then I felt a hand on my arm and turned.

He no longer smelled of soap and perfume but of

smoke and common sweat. But his face was as fair and rosy as ever it was before, and his honey-colored hair had been neatly trimmed by a monk's careful razor.

"Molly," he said, "it is time."

"Yes," I replied. "And Alaric—there is something I must tell you now."

❦ 24 ❧

The Abbot Elias

"I NEED YOU TO ARRANGE a meeting with the abbot. This afternoon, if possible."

Martin stared at me, dumbfounded. "I'm the almoner's boy," my brother said. "I don't make appointments with the abbot."

"Then ask the almoner to do it."

"No, Molls. No."

"I promise you, Elias will be glad to hear what we have to say. But the matter is delicate and secret, and cannot be bandied about the abbey."

He shook his head. "Even if I did have access to the abbot, which I do not, I would never bother him at such a time. He has heavy matters on his mind right now. Surely you can understand that."

"But these *are* heavy matters, Martin. Indeed, they are the very same."

"What? What is it you think is so urgent?"

"All right," I said. "I shall tell you. He said I might if there was no other way."

"He?"

"Yes. Now listen. You remember when Tobias and I came here, we traveled with a merchant from Austlind? We'd met him on the road. He'd been savaged by a dog and had lost all his money. We took pity on him and brought him with us so he could be cared for by the monks."

"Yes, Sebastian, I know all that. He was among the ones who survived the fire."

"Yes. Only none of that story was true. His name isn't really Sebastian."

"What is it, then?"

"It's Alaric." I looked him hard in the eyes. My brother blanched. "He's alive, Martin. Our rightful king. He is here, and in terrible danger."

Elias met us in his chambers, but only after he'd closed the shutters against prying eyes and sent away the novice who'd brought in the wine and the bread. Though it was midmorning, we talked by candlelight.

"Molly here tells me that you are not who you've been pretending to be but are instead our lost prince in disguise. Can this possibly be true?"

"Yes," he said. "I am Alaric, grandson of Mortimer the Bold, son of Godfrey the Lame, brother of Edmund the Fair, and the sole surviving descendant of the royal house of Westria."

He sat tall in his chair, hands resting on his knees, his gray eyes bright in the candlelight. I thought—and not for the first time—how unbearably handsome and noble he was despite the shabby clothes he wore. He carried himself with such dignity, and spoke so beautifully and with such authority, that no one could possibly have doubted he spoke the truth. Certainly Elias did not.

"My lord," the abbot said, bowing as low as his sizable paunch would allow, "you bring me more joy than you can possibly imagine. The message that was brought to us this morning—it was a blow, my lord. A heavy blow indeed. And now I learn you have been here all this time—and in our hospice, among the paupers."

"It's true. I was."

"It grieves me most terribly to hear it, Your Grace."

"There's no reason it should, Elias. I was cared for most capably by Brother Eutropious. As for the humble surroundings—they proved a most excellent lesson for me, and one I needed to learn. For if I am to rule, I must know my people. All of them, even the paupers."

"Very well said, my lord. Very princely indeed." Elias heaved a great sigh of satisfaction.

"I regret I could not declare myself sooner—to you or to my countrymen. I know there are many who have sorely grieved for me, thinking me dead and the kingdom lost. But I needed time to recover from my wounds; and I had to do it in secret, as I have powerful enemies who would gladly take advantage of my weakness.

"But now it seems I can wait no longer. Reynard forces my hand. And if I am to reveal myself and claim my right to the throne, I'm afraid I shall need some help from you."

"I will do everything within my power, my lord. You need only tell me what you require."

"Clothes befitting a prince, for a start. And a good horse, not skittish. I'll need messengers, quite a few—men you trust without question. I will write out the letter I wish to send. Then perhaps a few of your scribbling monks can get busy making copies—in a fair hand, on good vellum. When they are finished, I shall sign them. I'm afraid I have no seal."

"You may use mine if you wish. 'Twill come with some authority, though not much. It's better than none at all."

"I agree. Now, I shall also need a cart and a driver to escort Molly safely to Castleton—leaving today, if you can arrange it. There's important business she must do for me at Dethemere."

"Excuse me, Your Majesty," Elias said, "but perhaps you have forgotten that Reynard has occupied the castle?"

"Of course I have not forgotten. But Molly worked there for many years. The other servants will vouch for her."

"I see."

"My lord," I said, "Tobias was a carter in your brother's stables. And he wishes to go with me to keep me company and offer such help as I might need. He can handle the horses. There's no need of a driver."

"That may be," said Alaric, "but I was thinking more of protection. I'm glad Tobias will go with you, but I want the driver, too—someone rather menacing in appearance who knows how to use a sword."

"Excuse me again, sire," said Elias. "But if this is an urgent matter of great import—"

"It is. The whole enterprise is forfeit if she doesn't succeed."

"Then might it not be wiser to send someone . . . older? Someone more experienced? Someone—"

I saw impatience flash across Alaric's face. "Elias," he said, "the matter is secret. I cannot reveal it even to you. But understand this: no one but Molly can accomplish this task. And though she be young, and common, and a girl—I would lay my life and my kingdom in her hands without a second's thought."

"Ah," said the abbot, deeply embarrassed. "Then I shall find you a perfect monster to drive them to Castleton. He shall frighten small children and brigands alike."

"Excellent. Now I'm afraid I have no money whatsoever to pay you for any of this. Would a princely donation to the abbey suffice as soon as I am able?"

"Of course, Your Majesty. We would be most grateful."

"Now I'm going to write out a list of names for your messengers: men I feel sure will rally to my side and swear fealty to me as their sovereign lord. I shall ask each of them to gather such friends as are loyal and willing, and bring them here to the abbey in four days' time. It will not be an army exactly, but I hope for a goodly number of able men devoted to my cause. They may assemble here? You give your permission?"

"Well, yes. I am not sure how we shall manage to house and feed so many, but—"

"They can camp in the courtyard, and you can bring up food from the town. They won't be here long. Have I asked too much of you, lord abbot? Can you do it?"

"The scribbling monks and the messengers I can arrange myself. And Brother Jerome, our hosteler, will do his best to look after your people—so long as you don't expect a bed and a seat at table for every man. I shall have to apply to Bertram, our local lord, in the matter of the warhorse and the clothes. You will also need armor, I presume."

"No."

"No? You have some already?"

"I shall not need it."

"Ah. I assume then—I'm sorry if this is presumptuous, Your Highness—that you do not mean to actually fight yourself. I must say, I think that is wise, as you have been wounded, and are very young, and are not yet finished with your training in the arts of war."

"I am sixteen."

"Ah. Well then, there must be among your known supporters some man you particularly trust, one who can guide and instruct you in directing your army—help you come up with a battle plan, and see to the tactics, and so on? For though I have lived a quiet and secluded life, even I can see it is no easy thing to take a castle well manned by knights."

"I hope I shall not need to."

"You will not challenge Reynard, then?"

"Oh, I will challenge him. And though I am young—as you so kindly pointed out—I've spent many days lying upon that cot in your hospice thinking upon the matter. I may not be a knight, nor tested in battle; but I have read widely and deeply of the great kings of past ages, and of all that befell them and their kingdoms, and of war, and—"

"*Books*, my lord?"

"Yes, books."

"Oh, merciful heavens!"

"Elias—I am amazed that a learned man such as you would scorn the written word."

"I most assuredly do not. But my life is a spiritual one. Yours must be more . . . practical."

"And so I must learn useful skills, is that it? How to ride fast, and slice off a man's head with my sword?"

"Well, that is rather a gruesome way to put it, sire—but yes. And how, you know, to organize your troops, and . . . and whatever it is you must do in war. It is beyond me, I'm afraid."

"That's all in books too, Elias—and not just how such things are done in our country, and in our time, but how they've been done throughout the ages. By the Greeks, and the Romans, and the Persians, and the Parthians, and all the mighty kingdoms they fought against."

The abbot was speechless.

"And that's only the half of it. All the great events of the past are laid down in those pages. And new ideas to inspire the imagination, and great questions to ponder. How are we to imagine what we've never seen or experienced if we don't go to the past and learn from it?"

"But *Reynard*, my lord—will you fight him or not?"

"I hope to win a moral victory, for my claim is righteous and the people of Westria will rally to my side."

The abbot drew in a deep breath and slumped back in his chair, his arms slack, his eyes wide. "My lord," he said. "Do you think . . . are you saying . . . do you truly believe that Reynard of Austlind is just going to give you the throne?"

"It isn't his to give; it's mine by right."

Elias covered his mouth with a pudgy hand. He looked so utterly stupefied that Alaric broke into a hearty laugh. "I know my cousin better than you, lord abbot. And while it is true that I am young, and a bit of a dreamer, I assure you I am no fool."

"I . . . I'm sure you are not." The abbot looked down at his hands and picked distractedly at a fingernail. "But—oh, my prince, I do fondly hope you are right."

❦ 25 ❧

Kissing Elbows

LUKAS, OUR DRIVER, was a great brawny fellow with powerful hands and a face that just dared you to cross him. He was well armed, too, with both a sword and a dagger. As we rattled along the roadway, his head moved constantly left to right, searching the forest as if a band of brigands might be hiding behind every tree.

Before we left, Elias had given the man his orders: "I wish you to imagine," he said, "that you are carrying precious cargo: chests of gold, emeralds, diamonds, and rubies."

Lukas turned this over in his head and rubbed his nose with the side of his hand, emitting a little grunt.

"That is how I want you to drive: as if these are not mere servants with their basket of provisions but the king and queen of the realm with all their treasure. Do you understand me?"

"I do," he said.

"You will convey them safely to Castleton, with such haste as you can manage without overtaxing the horses. Then you will wait there at a meeting place of their choosing until they are ready to return."

Lukas grunted again—a man of few words he was—and we were off.

It was Tobias who'd suggested the meeting place. He said the Boar and Bristle was a respectable inn, clean and said to be well priced. Better still, it was near the west gate of the castle, so we could get there in a hurry. He knew all this because Castleton was his home. He'd lived in that very same neighborhood as a child.

This came as a shock to me. It made me realize that in all the years I'd known Tobias, and considered him my dearest friend, I'd never once thought to ask him about his life before the castle or anything regarding his family.

There are times when I do not like myself. This was one of them.

Was I so unbelievably selfish, thinking only of my

own life and my own problems? Yes, somewhat, but that wasn't the only reason. Might it be that since I'd left my own home so gladly, eager to start over in a happier place, I'd assumed everyone else felt the same? Yes, there was definitely some truth to that. And certainly Tobias never brought it up, had never mentioned his family, not once.

Still, that was no excuse.

"Tobias?" I said. "I didn't know you were born in the castle town."

He shrugged. "Well, I was."

"On the west side? Or across the river?"

"On the west, near the gate, in the very shadow of the castle walls."

"Is your family still there? Did you go to visit them sometimes, while we still lived at the castle?"

"No, Molly. They died in the pestilence, a long time ago."

"All of them?"

"Yes."

"I'm so sorry. I can't believe I never asked till now. I talked about myself and never bothered—"

"It's all right," he said.

"Were you already working at the castle, then, when they . . . when they died? I mean, you didn't catch the pestilence yourself, so you must—"

"No. I was there, at home. I took care of them when they got sick. And when they died, I washed their bodies and laid them out proper."

"Oh, Tobias," I said. "That's horrible. And you were only . . . ?"

"Eight."

I felt sick and didn't say anything for a while. Then a new thought came to me and made me glad.

"Tobias, would you like to say out their names, the way the abbot did in church? I thought that was nice, you know? Respectful. To remember them and say their names, and tell about how they were in life."

He looked at me, somehow managing to smile and look stricken at the same time. "All these years later?"

"Well, I would think, in a time of pestilence, there wouldn't be much in the way of proper good-byes."

"No," he said.

"Then why not now? Say their names. I want to hear them."

"All right," Tobias said.

Then nothing. I figured he was thinking.

"Angelica. My mother."

"Tell about her. What was she like?"

"She had yellow hair and she was tall. She sang while she cooked, and cleaned, and did her weaving. Those songs the little girls performed at the banquet—remember? They were my mother's songs, too. I recognized every one of them. It nearly made me weep."

It nearly made me weep, too, when he said this.

"She wrapped a cloth around her hand whenever she scrubbed a pot, to protect her knuckles from scrapes."

"Angelica," I said, just as Elias had in church. "May her soul rest in peace."

He took a deep breath so he wouldn't cry. "Matthew, my father. He was quiet, never said much. He was a cooper."

"Tell me what he looked like."

"Dark. He had a big nose and lots of hair. He had a good laugh."

"Good how?"

"It made you want to laugh with him."

"Like yours, then."

"I never thought of it. Yes, I suppose."

"Matthew," I said. "May he laugh in heaven."

Tobias was quiet for a while.

"Is that all?"

"No. Jacob, my brother. He was just a baby, always sickly."

"Did he cry a lot?"

"Yes. Mother carried him about, strapped to her

bodice with a shawl. He seemed to like it. He was quieter then."

"Anything else?"

"He was the first to die. It nearly broke Mother's heart."

"Jacob," I said. "May he rest in his mother's arms in paradise."

I waited. I did not want to ask again "Is that all?" I already knew it was not. I could tell by the look on Tobias's face: this was going to be the hardest one.

"Mary," he said.

"Your sister?"

"Yes. She was . . . ," and though he turned his head away, I could see that his face was contorted and that there were tears glistening in his eyes. "She was an angel child, the happiest creature that ever lived."

"Fair or dark?"

"Fair, with gray eyes, same as Prince Alaric has. Whenever I look at him, I think of her."

"What did she like to do?"

"She sang with Mother and danced in circles. And she kissed everyone and everything—the baby, the cat, my elbow."

"Your elbow?"

"She heard that saying once, you know: 'Well, kiss my elbow!' She got it into her head it was a good thing to do. We encouraged it because we thought it was funny."

"How old was she when—"

"Just turned four. She died last. It was only the two of us for a while, with Mother and Father laid out on the bed, and the baby nestled between them. Mary kept asking questions I couldn't answer, about why they were sleeping so long and when would Mama get up and make her porridge? I said they were just very tired. But it was hot, and soon they began to stink. I knew we had to leave; but they boarded up the houses, you know, when folk were struck down by the pestilence, so we couldn't go out and spread it about the town."

"Oh, Tobias!"

"I worked the boards off a back window, and we crawled out in the dark of night. We left the town, and went into the king's park, and hid among the trees. I brought food and blankets. I thought . . . I thought if we could get away from that place she would be all right; and I imagined a sort of life for us—how we would go to some cottage, and the people would welcome us and give me work to do. And they would dote on Mary as everyone did. . . ."

I waited.

"But she died. I buried her there. I dug the grave with a stick. It took me all day."

He waved me away with his hand: *Please don't ask anymore.*

"Mary," I said. "May she sing with the angels and kiss every elbow in heaven."

I hadn't meant to make him cry, but I had. I put my arms around him and rested my head upon his shoulder. We bounced along the road like that, in the back of a wagon, as the sun set gray in the west and it started to snow.

❧ 26 ❧

We Return
to the Castle

LUKAS DROVE THE HORSES HARD, and we arrived at Castleton well before vespers. We left him at the inn to make his arrangements and stable the horses, while we made haste toward the west gate of Dethemere Castle.

We waited in the guardhouse while enquiries were made as to whether any of the servants would vouch for us and whether they wished to take us back into service in our former positions. They did, right gladly. Indeed, everyone seemed pitifully grateful to have us. They were overburdened and understaffed. So many had fled; so few had returned.

It was strange to be back there again, for every-thing—and nothing—had changed. Reynard slept in the king's chamber now, and the guards on the ram-parts were from Austlind. But my bed was still in the storeroom, just as I'd left it, with my old work clothes folded and tucked beneath the pillow. The few coins I'd saved from my pay lay untouched in the apron pocket. Winifred's belongings were there beside mine, and I felt a stab of missing her—for all that she tossed in the night and kept me awake. I vowed to take her things with me when I went and to see that they got to her somehow.

The prince would arrange it, I felt sure.

The same cook still ruled the kitchen, but his staff was mostly new—green recruits from the town, not a fancy cook among them. Roasted meat, and boiled vegetables, and the occasional eel pie—that's all they made now. Any housewife could've done the same. Even our bread and ale were brought in from the town, as there was no one fit to run the bake-house or the brewery. It was a terrible comedown from the old days.

Several times when the cook was elsewhere, I tried the door to the silver closet. But it was always locked. Nor was Thomas anywhere to be seen. I supposed he'd fled on the night of the banquet like everybody else. Still, I couldn't imagine him abandoning his precious silver like that: the candlesticks, the platters, the cups, the saltcellar. The great hand basin.

At some point after the wolves left and the bodies had been carried off, someone must have gone into the hall to clear away the dishes. Then someone else, whatever such scullions as were to be found, would have washed them—and then what? Thomas had the keys to the silver closet, and there was no sign that anyone had smashed the door to gain entrance. So where would they have put it all: a banquet's worth of serving pieces?

I asked the cook, but he said he didn't know. I should stop asking questions and attend to my work.

I grew ever more anxious as each day passed. I'd been sent to destroy the bowl, but I didn't know where it was. Meanwhile, the prince's plans were unfolding, and he was still in danger. So far I had accomplished nothing.

But I held out one last hope, and that was the coronation. I knew how much planning went into such occasions. Any day now Reynard's steward was sure to remember the silver and send someone to make an inventory. They'd find it then, wherever it might be, and I'd come forward and offer to polish it.

It seemed so likely, and yet I waited in vain. No steward arrived. I spent my hours turning meat on a spit, or washing vegetables, or ripping the guts out of chickens.

And then, wonder of wonders, Thomas walked in.

"By the saints!" I cried. "I thought you'd gone away."

"What—and leave my silver?" He said it with a grin.

"Well, that did seem so unlikely."

"I haven't had occasion to be here for a while." He lowered his voice. "Much has changed, as you know."

"Yes." We locked eyes.

"But now we are back, both of us, and the silver must be attended to. It will be like old times."

"Yes," I said.

Not exactly, I thought.

Thomas went to the cook and said he needed my help with the polishing.

The cook said that was too bad, because Thomas couldn't have me. The cook could not do everything himself, now could he? Indeed, he couldn't spare a single hand—not one!—as there were ever more mouths to feed, the castle swelling daily with newly arrived knights, along with their squires, and servants, and whatnot, and no one in the kitchen knew what to do—they were absolute fools, every one of them except me. I thought he would weep with frustration.

"King Reynard," Thomas said, "has asked to have his meals, humble though they are, presented on proper serving pieces, as is seemly in a royal hall. And with the coronation only weeks away, you can imagine the work that lies ahead of us."

"Of course I know that!" the cook wailed, wiping angry tears from his cheeks and stamping his foot with fury. "You think I don't know that?"

"Whether you know it or not, those are his instructions. No one has touched the silver since—"

"Fine! Polish away, Thomas. But why must you take her too?"

"This girl is my assistant. She's highly trained. 'Tis a positive sin to put a valuable servant to turning a spit by the fire. You shall just have to find a replacement."

With that he turned away and guided me toward the silver closet. Behind us I heard something smash against the flagstones. Thomas chose not to notice.

He calmly unlocked the door, went into the room, and lit the candles.

"I only just heard you'd returned. I was surprised, Molly—and glad."

I didn't like lying to Thomas and so I only smiled. Let him think I was glad to be there. At least I hadn't said it.

He opened a cupboard and got out the mortar and pestle, then the bag of chalk and the flagon of rainwater.

"I cannot speak to the quality of the food they will serve at the coronation banquet"—here he cast a scornful glance in the direction of the cook—"but the table shall be as grand as ever it was in Edmund's time, if we have to work night and day to accomplish it."

He started bringing out some of the larger pieces. I went to work as of old, mixing the chalk and water, grinding it fine with the pestle.

"Thomas?" I asked in an offhand way. "Do you serve Reynard now as your liege lord?"

He stared at me, astonished. "No, child! My allegiance has never changed."

"Oh," I said. "I am glad to hear it."

"How could you doubt it?"

"I didn't—not really. But you spoke with such

eagerness just now, about making everything beautiful for the coronation. And you called him 'King Reynard.' He isn't king yet, Thomas, not until he's crowned."

"But he is, child. He's king of Austlind."

"Oh." I blushed. "Of course."

"And as to setting a fine table—I have cared for this silver all of my life. And so long as I am here, the castle shall maintain its standards, whoever rules."

I smiled. How very like Thomas that was!

We spent the better part of the day on wine flagons, and bread trays, and serving bowls. They'd all been polished for Elinor's wedding and had not been used since. Many only needed a little buffing up. We progressed nicely.

I tried to appear calm, but my mind was all agitation, considering any number of different strategies for how I was to proceed. But every plan seemed to run aground on the very same rock: Thomas. There was no other way. I would have to tell him.

"Thomas?" I said.

"Yes?"

"The bowl, the great hand basin—"

"We shall get to it soon enough. I don't suppose you heard about the saltcellar."

"No. What?"

"It was knocked off the table when . . . well . . ."

"Oh."

"Several other pieces were damaged, too: a couple of bowls and trays and a very special wine flagon. But the saltcellar is the real tragedy. The crystal salt dish was smashed, and one of the lions came loose. There were dents as well, and the base is askew. I took it to a silversmith here in the town to see if he could repair it. But I have little hope it will be ready in time for the coronation, and even then I cannot speak to the quality of the man's work."

"Well, yes, that's a pity," I said. "But the bowl, Thomas—there is something about it I must tell you."

He stopped his work and turned to look at me curiously.

"You will have to keep your mind open to what I'm about to say. It may be difficult to believe."

"I shall make an effort." He tried to suppress a grin.

I leaned across the table and said, "Thomas, the prince still lives! He escaped that night, with Tobias and me, and has been hiding all this time while he recovers from his wounds."

"That cannot be!" he said. "It's known for certain that he drowned."

"No," I said. "That was a lie. I saw him only a few days ago."

"Wait." He got up and shut the door, then returned to his seat on the bench. "You must keep your voice low, Molly."

"Sorry."

"I am most amazed to hear this. Where is Alaric now? Will he come to Dethemere?"

"I cannot talk of his plans. But he sent me here on a particular mission. It is vital to his cause, and, well . . . it has to do with the bowl."

"The bowl? How can it have anything—?"

"You have heard of the curse that has plagued the royal family?"

"Oh, Molly, child, that's nothing but peasant superstition. Surely you don't—"

"No, it's true. You were there at the banquet. You saw those unnatural wolves and how knowing and particular they were as to who they killed. There's an evil enchantment on the royal family. And I'm sorry, Thomas, but the great hand basin—beautiful as it is, and as much as you love it—that vessel carries the curse."

He was incredulous. "Truly, child, whatever gave you such a peculiar notion?"

"The bowl did, Thomas. It speaks to me. It grows warm in my hands when I touch it, and it hums and buzzes beneath my fingers. Soon I begin to hear a voice, and it urges me to listen, then it shows me all manner of strange little scenes. They're confusing, and all jumbled about, but I understand enough. The thing was made with evil intent and was filled with a hundred curses. Most of them are still there, Thomas, and they grow stronger every year. If the bowl is not destroyed soon, those curses will murder Alaric, just as they did all the others. I'm not mad, Thomas—truly. I told the prince everything, and *he* believes me."

Thomas looked away, lost in thought. The thinking went on for some time. Then he turned back and looked at me, his expression solemn. "And I believe you also," he said, "for I have noted some strangeness about the bowl myself. It made me uneasy, and so I gave it to you to polish. I'm sorry, child. That was wrong of me."

"Oh, Thomas—I don't care about that!"

"What's more—though it is a great and precious

work of art—I shall help you destroy it if you so wish."

"I do. Oh, Thomas, I wish it very much!"

"Good. Then have you considered how to go about it?"

"I have thought of little else: smashing it with a mallet, melting it down in the fire—"

"No," he said. "That would only destroy the bowl, not the enchantment. Think of a deadly plant: if you crush it, will it not still be just as noxious as before? And in crushing it, won't you just release the poisonous juices out where they can do harm?"

"Yes, I see that. But I can't think of any other way to go about it."

"The voice you hear—you say it comes from the bowl?"

"Yes. It keeps calling to me, warning of a plot against the king and asking for my help."

"That's odd. I mean no offense, child, but you are only a girl and—"

"I know. Tobias said much the same thing: would it not have been more helpful if the voice had called to Edmund and told him to beware? Or to the captain of the guard?"

"Exactly."

"Though what anyone could have done against those wolves I cannot think—even the captain of the guard—whether they were warned beforehand or not."

"Alaric managed to escape."

"Yes, that's true. Twice, actually. There was a fire at the . . . in the place where he is staying. And no, it wasn't an ordinary fire. It was no more natural than the wolves were."

"Then the prince is fortunate indeed."

"He says I'm his good-luck charm."

"Perhaps you are, child, though the source of your power is—once again, I mean no affront—not at all evident to me. Still, as you seem to have protected Alaric thus far and the bowl calls out for your help, I have to believe it will guide you now and teach you the way to reach down into its heart and destroy the evil within."

"Guide me how?"

"I don't know. I suppose you should polish it as you did before and wait until it speaks. Then you can ask. We'll do it tonight, when all is quiet and no one is around. All right?"

"Oh, Thomas," I said, "I'm so glad I don't have to do this alone."

"So am I," he said. "Though it really is a terrible pity."

"A pity?"

"Yes. Such a fine piece of silver."

And then I saw that he was joking.

❦ 27 ❧

A Dazzle
of Silver Mist

I WRAPPED MY FEW POSSESSIONS, along with Winifred's, into a tidy parcel. Then I slipped it under my pillow, ready to leave at a moment's notice. That done, I went in search of Tobias, eager to tell him the news—that Thomas had reappeared and had promised to help, and that we would attempt to destroy the bowl that very night. If all went well, we could leave the castle first thing the following morning.

"I'm glad," he said, "for I was beginning to worry. There's been a steady stream of knights and wagons coming into the castle—the wagons filled with food, weapons, and armor. Reynard is preparing for a siege,

Molly; I'm sure of it. And if we don't leave soon we'll be trapped here, in the enemy camp, of no use to Alaric at all."

"You think Reynard knows about the prince?"

"He must. It's not an easy thing to keep secret, what with all those messages being sent out and so many men on the move."

"Listen," I said. "If things don't go well tonight, you must leave tomorrow anyway. You can go to the prince and tell him what happened. There's no sense in both of us—"

"Oh, stop it, Molly! Why should you fail? You've been called to do this thing, so there must be a way. The Guardian will tell you. Surely he knows what must be done."

"Oh, there's nothing sure about it, Tobias. Nothing sure at all. But I very much hope you are right."

❧ ❧

It was dark and still throughout the castle as I tiptoed up the stairs to the kitchen. I had taken off my shoes so as not to make any noise, and the stone floors were cold against my feet. Perhaps that was why I trembled.

Thomas looked up as I entered the room, but he didn't say a word. He just met my eyes, then glanced down again. On the table, shining in the light of the candles, was the silver bowl.

I sat on the bench before it, my heart pounding. I reached out and touched the rim.

"Does it feel warm?" Even though we were alone and the door was shut, he spoke in a whisper.

"Not yet," I said. "It usually happens when I'm polishing it—the inside part, where the carving is deep."

"Yes, of course. That's how it was for me. Here. You may proceed." He'd already made the paste, and the cloth was already damp. Still I hesitated.

"It's like sticking my hands into a basketful of serpents."

"I know. I wish I could do it in your stead, but—"

"I understand." I touched my chest again, feeling the silver disk warm beneath my gown. It had become a habit of late, something I did when I was frightened or sad. It always made me feel better. Finally I took up the cloth and began.

Thomas watched as I worked, making patient circles with the paste and the cloth.

He moved one of the candles closer. This brought out the pattern, casting shadows in the deep places, causing the raised parts to shimmer and tremble in the flickering light. I rubbed it with my cloth and stared till I was almost in a trance.

"Anything yet?"

"No," I said, and could hear the edge in my voice. "I'm sorry, Thomas, but when you speak to me, you break my concentration."

"I won't ask again," he said.

I returned to my work, driving everything from my mind but the task at hand, and at last the silver began to quicken and grow warm; I felt that humming of invisible bees beneath my fingertips. Now the pattern was breaking up, writhing and flowing in the candlelight. I leaned in closer to study it.

Thomas didn't move an eyelash, but he knew.

The shallow bowl seemed to grow deeper now. I was looking down into a great, wide space—a rutted, grassy meadow encircled by a fogbank, beyond which nothing could be seen. Even within the meadow things were not clear or distinct, for the air was filled with a gauzy silver haze. And there in the center, gazing up at me, was a small figure made entirely of silver: the Guardian; it had to be.

"You came!" said the familiar voice.

"Yes."

"Oh, bless you!"

Then he made a quick, strange motion with his hands; and after that I lost myself entirely. I was lightheaded and queasy. There was a roaring in my ears, like a powerful wind; and around me there was nothing but a dazzling silver mist. I was tumbling through clouds, the air cool and moist against my skin; and I fell slowly, almost floating, as in water.

I wondered if this was what dying was like.

❦ 28 ❧

Uncle

THERE WAS GRASS BENEATH MY FINGERS. I opened
my eyes and saw clouds, but they were whirling about in
a most unnerving way. The spinning made my stomach
lurch, so I closed my eyes against the dizziness, and after
a time it passed. I rolled over then, pushing myself into a
sitting position so I could look around.

It was the place I'd just seen in my vision—the rutted meadow of wild grass, disappearing on all sides
into dense fog. And everything was silver except for
me, even the delicate blades of grass. But why did it all
feel so familiar, this strange, winding landscape with
its high and low places? I felt sure I'd seen it before,
perhaps even been there.

And then it came to me—of course it was familiar. I'd polished every inch of it. I was inside the bowl!

Oh, this was not what I'd expected, not at all! I'd come to the castle to smash the bowl, or melt it down, or sommat like that. Then when Thomas had explained why that wouldn't work and said I must ask the Guardian what to do, I'd convinced myself that the Guardian would know some clever magic trick, some enchantment or charm to wash the evil away.

I had not thought I'd have to fight the curses myself, in person.

True, I was ever quick with a slap and a kick; I'd been in my share of street brawls. I'd even dispatched two demon wolves. But those were mere trifles compared to a whole pack of curses. I will not lie about it: I lost every shred of hope and courage then. I put Alaric out of my mind. All I wanted was to run away. But where? There was nothing around me but grass and fog. I sat there for a long time, feeling wretched, weeping in pity for my own poor self.

At some point I noticed the Guardian. He was kneeling quietly beside me, his hands folded in his lap, his expression full of sympathy and concern. I left off crying and wiped my face.

"You're incredibly brave to have come here," he said. "Not many would have done it."

"No," I said. "Not brave at all. I just fell in. And now that I'm here, I'm terrified."

He took one of my hands and clasped it in both of his. It surprised me how soft and warm they were. I felt his kindness flow into me, like good physic. "So am I, Molly dear—very much afraid. But the touch of your hand gives me comfort and hope."

"Yes," I said. "I can feel it, too."

"We're linked to each other, that's why. When your grandfather made me, he tempered the silver with his blood, as he did with his Loving Cups—for he himself was the source of all the magic. That makes us blood relatives. I'd be honored if you'd call me Uncle."

"All right, I will—Uncle. Most gladly."

"Good. Now, can you rise? Are you recovered from your fall?"

"Yes. I feel better now. You've taken my pains away."

"Then follow me. We only have a little time. They're in the forest now, sleeping. But come morning they'll wake; and as the fog lifts, we'll start to see them. We must be ready."

He led me along a winding pathway till we came to a circular platform, smooth and perfectly round. I remembered that too from when I'd polished the bowl: a perfect little disk, right in the center, so unlike the wild pattern that swirled around it.

"This is the door," he said, taking his place upon it like a soldier at the ramparts. "It's best not to leave it unguarded. And we need to keep watching the perimeter, too. Usually they sleep at night, but they can be tricky. A time or two I trusted to that and allowed myself to rest. As you know, a few escaped."

Already the fog was breaking up. I began to see the distant shape of silver trees, silver vines drooping low from their boughs, sparkling with drops of silver dew—but nothing moved within.

"Will it be a common fight, Uncle, with weapons and such? Or something strange and magical?"

A bitter little laugh. "No weapons," he said, "or at least not proper ones." He leaned down and picked up a pair of sticks that were lying in the grass. They were long and straight, branches broken from silver trees and sharpened at the tips. "This is all we have. I made them myself. But they're strong and sharp. Better than nothing."

"My grandfather charged you with the care of a hundred curses—and he didn't even give you a sword?"

"I didn't need one. They were just harmless infants back then."

"But—?"

"I was meant to let them out, you see, one each day

or so. If I'd done as I was bid, it would have been over in less than a year, with little harm done. But I couldn't bear to watch the child suffer." He paused and hung his head. "I didn't know they could grow up."

"Oh, Uncle!"

"I'm glad your grandfather didn't live to see it. He thought he was so clever when he was making them, you know. Such innocent little mishaps, such comical names he gave them: Tummy-Trouble, Cold-Porridge, Tangled-Up, Little-Nibble." He sighed. "They're not funny anymore."

All the time I'd been there, the light had been quite dim. But now a shadow fell over our little world and it grew darker still, as when a thunderstorm is nigh. We looked up. The sky was dense with clouds, but here and there were darker spots. They formed a shape—rather like the man-face you see on the moon. It moved, then, and there was a disturbance in the clouds. A figure came tumbling through them, arms and legs flailing.

"Thomas!" I cried, and took off running along the raised pathways, jumping over ditches, until I reached the spot where he lay. "Are you all right?" I thought about the pain of my own fall—and I was young; Thomas was an old man.

"I think so," he said, gasping. "Just had the breath knocked out of me."

"Shall I help you up?"

He thought about it. "Yes," he said. "All right. But slowly, child. Gently. That's it." He stood for a moment, one hand resting on my shoulder for balance, gazing around him. Then he gave a soft little laugh of amazement. "We're inside the bowl, Molly!"

"Yes. And I'm right glad you came, for we shall have to fight them, Thomas, with nothing but a couple of homemade lances. But now we are three. It begins to seem possible that we can do it."

"Indeed," he said. "All things are possible now."

And then—so unexpected!—he took me in his arms, tenderly, as a father would hold a beloved child. He even stroked my hair. "Molly," he said, "sweet little Molly."

He'd never done such a thing before—nor would I have expected him to. I was his servant, after all, and common, and a child. But I was his ally now, with a terrible battle ahead of us. He was treating me as his equal. I felt honored, and proud . . . and a little uncomfortable.

"Truly," Thomas said, "I am sorry about this. But I swore an oath, and I cannot turn from it now. Please understand, child, I never meant you any harm."

"*Harm*, Thomas?"

His hand was under my hair, searching for the

chain. I tried to pull away, but he'd recovered from his fall quite amazingly, and his grip was very strong. Then he gave the necklace a powerful tug. I felt it bite deep into the skin of my neck, like to choke me. At last the chain snapped and Thomas released me, pushing me away from him so that I stumbled into a ditch.

I watched as the disk came off the chain and went flying, landing in the grass. I saw Thomas pick it up. And then he was running away in the direction of the forest.

I climbed out of the ditch and saw that Uncle was nearly upon me. He had brought both of the sticks. I'd left mine behind in my excitement.

"I thought you meant to kill him," he said. "I thought you had a plan."

I just shook my head. "I don't understand, Uncle. Why did he do that?"

"He's the *one*, Molly. I showed it to you in the visions, remember? He swore his oath to Gertrude, then he ordered your grandfather to make the bowl and murdered him after."

"Oh, heaven help me, Uncle." I wailed. "You might have *shown me his face*!"

I grabbed the extra stick from his hand and I was off again, winding my way across the meadow, along the raised pathways, over the channels, in the direction of the forest. "Thomas!" I shouted as I ran. "Don't you dare!"

He was already into the trees by then, half hidden by the fog. But I could just see him turn and look at me.

"You will not harm the prince!" I said, wild with rage. "Not so much as a toe or an eyelash. I will not allow it!"

He smiled. "I'm afraid you have no power to forbid me anything. Not anymore." He held up the silver disk. "I'm sorry, Molly, but you're nothing but a common scullery maid now."

Then he disappeared into the mist.

❦ 29 ❧

Strong Point,
Weak Point

"WHEN WILL THEY START coming out?"

I meant to sound calm, but I could hear the trembling in my voice, for I'd been deeply shaken by Thomas's betrayal. Was anyone to be trusted? Who would turn on me next? Uncle? Tobias?

"We'll see them soon," Uncle said, gently resting his hand on my shoulder. "I'm afraid he went in there to wake them and tell them the portal is open." He sighed. "Whenever I stray from your grandfather's plan, everything goes awry. But I had no choice. I had to open it to let you in."

"So now the curses can escape?"

"If we don't kill them first."

"Can't you just close the portal?"

"No. Not until they're all gone: dead or into the world. Your coming here, our need to fight the curses, Thomas—none of that was anticipated; they were never part of the plan."

"That's very bad news, Uncle."

"Yes," he said. "Now listen, my dear. I've been with these creatures my whole life. I am familiar with all of them, their characters and their weaknesses. Likewise, they have known me since they were infants. I am as common to them as the grass and the trees; they don't consider me a threat. Once the killing starts, of course, that will likely change. But until it does, we may use those things to our advantage. And, Molly, I think we are about to begin. Over there, at the forest's edge. Do you see it?"

His eyes were better than mine. A silver figure on a silver background is hard to make out. But then I caught the movement against the trees.

"Yes, I see it now. It looks like a dandelion puff."

It seemed to hover in the air, which was odd since it had no wings. Then it came closer and I saw its long, delicate legs, eight or ten of them, like those of a giant spider. It was unsettling the way it crept along— insectlike, very fast—but it didn't seem particularly menacing.

"Don't let it deceive you," Uncle warned. "It is not so innocent as it appears." And just as he said it, the creature opened its enormous mouth, lined top and bottom with a double row of razor-sharp teeth, and let out a menacing hiss. I couldn't tell if it meant to threaten us or if that was just its common way.

"I think it knows," Uncle said. "Thomas must have told them I was not their kindly Guardian any-more. Let's split up and approach it from opposite sides. But, Molly, it's more likely to turn on you than on me, so if you see a chance to attack, you must go ahead and take it. And be quick on your feet if it starts coming at you."

All right, I thought as we crept toward it:

Weak point: it has spindly legs.

Strong point: it's fast.

Strong point: those teeth.

I touched my chest out of habit, forgetting that the necklace wasn't there, and felt the familiar surge of elation, and confidence, and strength. But I didn't have time to consider just then how very odd that was—for the creature was drawing closer now, dancing across the pathways with surprising grace and alarming speed.

And I realized our plan wouldn't work. To attack it from the side, I'd have to get in close enough to strike, then keep pace with it while I aimed my lance—but it was too quick footed for that. I needed a different strategy.

So I chose a spot where the ground was even and gripped my lance tight. Then I growled. It heard me and turned, scuttling straight in my direction. I judged its speed and made a quick calculation: I had maybe three seconds. When it was almost upon me, I jumped to the side, then squatted low and swung my stick under it, hard.

The fragile legs shattered just as I'd hoped, and the body pitched forward onto the ground, rolling into one of the gullies. There it lay, snapping and hissing and throwing itself about. I was afraid it might somehow work itself out of the ditch and come at me with those teeth, but I took the chance and crept closer. Choosing my moment, I lunged with my stick.

It collapsed like an empty wineskin—and then it began to melt. First it was thick, like molten silver, then thinner, like rainwater. Finally it soaked into the ground and was gone.

Uncle came up beside me and wrapped his arm around my shoulders.

"It just . . . disappeared."

"Yes. You destroyed the curse; its spirit is gone. What remained was only silver, and that has melted back into the bowl."

I was feeling exceedingly pleased with myself—Molly the Giant Killer! I turned to Uncle to crow a little but saw that his attention was elsewhere. Wordlessly he spun me around.

It was a serpent, or much like one, though it didn't slither on the ground. It danced and flickered through the air as an eel does in water. At times you could see it—indeed it seemed to glow bright from within—then at others it disappeared from sight. It darted and flashed across the meadow, and I thought for a moment how beautiful it was. But then of course—my grandfather was a great artist.

Unfortunately there were no weak points this time.

It danced ever higher and higher. Now it considered the clouds. It was remembering the portal. This was the end of it, then, for we could not reach up there where it was, and soon it would disappear—through the clouds, out into the bowl, to work its evil against the prince.

"Ague!" Uncle boomed. "Come see what I have for you!"

It twisted in the air and dived down, came close, then wriggled back up again.

"You'll like it, Ague. I know you will. Won't you come and see?"

Again it swam down to where we stood; but this time it stayed in front of Uncle, pulsing in the air, shimmering, coming and going from sight. The head, I saw now, was not like that of a serpent but birdlike, with a curved, sharp beak.

"Look," Uncle said, holding out his hands, cupped together. The creature trembled with excitement.

Uncle didn't have to say it; I knew what I had to do. As he slowly opened his hands, the serpent all attention, I gauged the broadest part of its body, then aimed my lance and struck. It collapsed and slowly began to lose its form, turning to molten silver. Even in death it shimmered in the sunlight.

Sunlight? How long had I been here? Could it already be dawn?

No, I realized, it couldn't. We were in the bowl, and the bowl was in a windowless room, and the door to the room was shut. The only light came from the candles on the table, and—

I looked at the sky; and there through the clouds I

saw Tobias, looking down at me, holding a candle.

"The large toad, Molly!" Uncle shouted.

"Behind you!" Tobias warned.

I turned. It was approaching with great, heavy leaps, ponderous and ungainly. Its body sloshed about as though it were filled with water. And on each of its three, long, serpentine necks sat a ghastly toad head, each with a mouth filled with tiny teeth and a pair of bulbous eyes. It ignored Uncle. It was only interested in me.

Weak point: thin necks.

Weak point: it's awkward and slow.

"How do I get in?" Tobias called.

"Get us some weapons, then just lean over. You'll fall in."

The toad was weaving its necks back and forth, in and out. I couldn't think why.

Weak point: the heads keep moving and are looking in different directions.

Three mouths opened; forked tongues explored the air. I menaced it with my stick, distracting it while Uncle crept up from behind.

Then he pierced the thing and it deflated as they all did, oozing rivers of silver blood, beginning its inexorable return to the heart of the silver bowl.

The light had dimmed now. Tobias had gone in

search of weapons. We both looked up expectantly.

"Who was that?" Uncle asked.

"Tobias," I said, "someone who's always there when I need him."

⊰ 30 ⊱

Buried

TOBIAS WAS STRONG and famously quick, but there'd been no time to make him a lance. All he had was the cook's boning knife. And though it was long and wickedly sharp, he'd have to get in close to strike. It was horribly dangerous.

I offered him my stick. I suggested we take turns. After all, he'd brought a knife for each of us. I didn't need two weapons.

But he refused. "I've got longer arms than you," he said. "And besides, the knife suits me."

I looked at him hard. "Don't you die on me, Tobias!" I said. "I couldn't bear it."

He only smiled.

I explained how it helped to use the demons' weaknesses against them. He nodded as I said it, and agreed it was a good idea, but that really wasn't his way. Oh, I'm sure he took a quick look first to see how best to proceed, but mostly he just ran straight at them. It was chilling to watch him do it. He was in with the knife and out again before most of them knew what had happened. He killed more that way than Uncle and I did with our strategy, but he took such dreadful chances. Already he was scratched and bleeding.

More of them had started coming out of the forest now, no longer one at a time but in clusters.

"I think we ought to separate," Uncle said. "Spread out across the meadow. That way they can't take us all at once."

"Oh, must we, Uncle?" I'd come to count on working with him. We pulled together like a well-matched team of oxen; we thought each other's thoughts.

"It's best," he said.

Tobias nodded agreement.

I gave a little sigh of dismay. I didn't like it, not at all. But apparently I'd completed my apprenticeship, moving up to journeyman curse-fighter. Would I become master of my craft by the end of that long night?

Reluctantly I agreed and began to walk away from the others.

"Molly!" Tobias called after me.

"What, Tobias?" I called back.

"Don't you die on me! I couldn't bear it."

I smiled. He knew how to lift my spirits.

We each fought our own separate battles after that. From time to time, as safety allowed, I would search out Uncle and Tobias, make sure they were still standing. When I saw that they were, it always gladdened my heart and gave me the courage to go on.

But now, having fought one creature after the other for hours with scarcely a moment of rest, working my muscles, working my brain—I had finally reached my limit. I was utterly spent, so worn I actually staggered as I walked. I wanted nothing so much as to lie down on the soft grass and sleep. As there was no danger just then, I shut my eyes. Only for a moment.

More than a moment it must have been, for how else could they have slipped up on me like that? Now as I opened my eyes, I saw they were alarmingly close, one on either side of me. I was trapped between them.

Most fearsome was the feral dog. Its head was massive, and it snarled and snapped at me, its eyes glittering bright. It moved like a rabid animal in a jerky, stumbling way.

On my other side—I knew not what to call it. An enormous, oozing silver bubble. A monster-slug.

Weak point, Slug: slow and soft. Appears to be blind. No teeth, no claws.

Weak point, Dog: none that I can see.

I went for the dog.

It crouched, growling deep within its throat, drawing back its lips, baring its hideous teeth. But I stood my ground, teasing it with my stick. It froze for a moment and appeared to be thinking. Suddenly it sprung to the side and gripped the lance in its powerful jaws just short of the point, then shook it, trying to wrench it from my hands. As we struggled, I slowly lowered the end of the stick till the dog's head was almost resting on the ground. It couldn't lunge from that position. It was twisted to the side, one shoulder down. The angle was perfect. With all the strength I still possessed, I jammed the lance forward. I had hoped it would slide through its teeth and enter the dog's chest.

But the creature was stronger than I knew. It gripped the shaft even tighter in its jaws. And so I abandoned the stick altogether and sprang suddenly, drawing out my knife. But the creature was quick, too. It released the lance and rose to attack, jaws open wide. It was as close as a heartbeat. I felt its heavy breath as I drove in the knife.

It was a good thing the curses died quickly, the very

second you struck them—for had the dog lingered in its death throes, it would have killed me.

I waited a couple of seconds more to make sure it was dead. Then I turned to attend to the slug.

I saw in a flash that I'd made the wrong decision. I should have killed the slug first—it would have been quick and easy. Instead, I'd given it the leisure to make its slow advance. Now there wasn't even time to step away, for already it had trapped my feet and was crawling over me. It was enormous; and soon I was buried beneath it, unable to move, or breathe, or see. Its terrible weight was crushing me—pressing into my face, pinning my arms at my side, and oh, the horrible, gagging smell!

If I could only turn my head a little, enough to capture a pocket of air! But I couldn't. I was going to die.

In a foggy corner of my mind I noted that the weight of the monster was less heavy than before—though I still couldn't move; and its foul, slimy body still covered my face, pressing my nose flat, forcing my lips hard against my teeth.

I was on the verge of losing consciousness when it came to me, the reason it was getting lighter: my left hand still gripped the knife, and the blade was pointed upward. I had killed the creature, quite by accident, and it was dying right on top of me.

I could feel the weight growing lighter still. Maybe there was a chance now. I had to try—my body was screaming for air. Gathering all my strength, I tucked in my chin and tried to turn my head to the side. It hurt my neck something awful and scraped the skin on my face, but my head moved a little. Then a bit more, and at last, with the corner of my mouth, I sucked in a great, gasping breath—foul, foul, disgustingly foul!— but it was air.

I continued to lie there for a long time after that till the thing had melted away, leaving nothing behind but its horrible stink. Even then I didn't move. I wasn't even sure I could. I remember thinking—hoping—that nothing truly dreadful would creep up on me while I lay there gasping, staring at the sky.

I felt strangely peaceful. There was nothing above me but mist.

And then there was Thomas.

He reached down, and for a moment I confusedly thought he was offering me a friendly hand up. Instead, he pulled me sharply to my feet, twisting my arm behind me, causing me to drop the knife. His face was unrecognizable, contorted with grief, and rage, and terrible disappointment.

"I should have killed you the day you came back," he said. "I've known who you were since the night of the banquet. I recognized the necklace. But I thought to play a subtle game with you, trick you and the Guardian into opening the bowl so that I could free the curses. I regret that now." He gave another jerk, and I thought for a moment that my arm would separate from the shoulder.

"Do you know how long I've waited—waited in shame because I'd failed at my task? Forty-six years! And then, when it was almost over, nearly finished— you had to come along and destroy the curses!"

I clawed at his face with my free hand, but he grabbed my wrist and pinned that one behind me too. Then he slid his knife out of its sheath—not his knife, I saw, but the prince's dagger, with the emerald set into the pommel. He held the blade to my throat.

"But by God, Molly," Thomas said, "I shall kill you now."

I felt the steel cutting into my flesh; I struggled to pull away. It was hard to believe an old man could be that strong. And then I heard a thud; and Thomas twitched, his head and shoulders jerking back, loosening his grip on my hands enough that I could free one arm. I shoved him away from me.

There stood Uncle with his stick. Another swing, another terrible blow, and Thomas fell to his knees, his head lolling forward. Uncle raised the stick again.

You'd think I'd be glad, but it sickened me. This was a man I'd known for years. I'd thought well of him. I'd trusted him with my life.

Now I watched him die.

He didn't melt away as the others had. He just lay there broken and ruined, covered in blood.

I looked at Uncle through my tears.

"Thomas was evil," he said.

"But he was a person."

"Yes. And he had a soul, and education, and was born to privilege. Yet he brought about the death of all those people just because he loved the lady Gertrude and had sworn to avenge her wrongs—because she'd been overlooked, because her father would not make her his heir. For that he chose the path of murder. Teething-Pains, and Slimy-Worm, and all the rest— they never had a choice but to be what they were. I mourn for them a hundred times more than I do for Thomas."

"It's horrible all the same."

"Yes. And I'm glad I could do it so you wouldn't have to."

And then I let him hold me, and pat my head, and say comforting things. I felt his good magic flowing through me again and wanted to stay there forever. But soon he broke the embrace and looked me squarely in the eyes.

"It's over now," he said. "They're all gone. It's time for my spirit to escape."

"No!"

"Molly, I've been in this place, keeping watch, since your mother was a babe. Don't you think I've earned my rest?"

"But I'll never see you again!"

"I know. And I shall miss you most horribly. But my spirit will escape whether I will it or not. It's how I was made. Come now. Tobias needs our help."

He lay in the grass, his hand pressed against his head, blood seeping between his fingers. Uncle squatted down and touched him on the shoulder. "Tobias," he said, "you have to get up now."

He tried, then groaned and lay back again.

"Tobias!" Uncle said, more urgently this time. "I have finished with my task. Now my spirit must escape. When it does, the bowl will close forever. You must leave this place, and quickly."

"But how, Uncle?"

He paused. "I don't know. None of this was part of the plan. But you came in through the clouds. Perhaps . . ." He let out a little gasp. "Oh!" he said. "I can feel my spirit rising even now."

And sure enough, Uncle began to soften around

the edges. He was melting just as the curses had. And at the same moment, it began to grow darker. I looked up and saw that the circle of light was growing smaller and smaller.

Then from far above us, for the very last time, I heard the old, familiar voice.

"The trapdoor!" it called.

And then the world went dark.

⚛ 31 ⚛

An Eye-Catching Pair

I WAS SITTING ON A BENCH. I could feel a table in front of me.

I must be back in the pantry, then—and not in Limbo, or some anteroom of heaven or hell. The candles had just gone out, that was all.

Had I dreamed it?

"Tobias?" I whispered into the darkness.

Nothing.

"Are you there?"

Nothing.

With trepidation: *"Thomas?"*

Still no answer.

I explored the tabletop, brushing the edge of the bowl—cold now, as any normal thing made of metal ought to be when it had lain for hours in a chilly room— then pulling my hand away. I did not like to touch it.

I slipped my legs over the bench, got to my feet, and felt around for a candlestick. I found one, knocked it over, but caught it before it rolled onto the floor. Then, candle in hand, I felt my way toward the far wall, located the latch, and opened the door.

Ah, light! Not a lot of it, but compared to the coffin-like pantry, the kitchen was dazzling bright. I carried the candle over to the hearth, walking slowly—hobbling is more like it, for I ached in every corner of my body.

With a poker I nudged one of the embers from under the fire-cover and set the wick against it till it caught. Then I saw, by the light of the candle, that my hands and arms were all over scratched and bleeding. My gown was torn and stained with blood.

Not a dream, then.

Carefully guarding the flame with my hand, I went back to the pantry; but still no one was there. *Oh, Tobias,* I thought—*did I leave you behind? Did you die in there?* I began to tremble and couldn't stop the shaking. And so I went back to the kitchen and sat upon the hearth, weeping and soaking up what little warmth there was to be had. I felt so unbearably alone.

And then I heard a moan coming from the pantry. I hurried back and searched every corner of the room. But still it was empty. I must have imagined it—that groan.

Except that now it came again.

Candle in hand, I squatted down and peered beneath the table. And then, "Oh, Tobias!" I said. "Are you all right?"

"Iyanntano," he answered.

"You don't know?"

"Unh hnh."

I got up again, and lit all the candles, and set them in a row on the floor. Then I crawled under the table and knelt beside him.

"Where does it hurt the most?"

Was that a laugh? Good.

"Everrrrrr . . ."

"Everywhere?"

"Unh."

Oh, he looked dreadful, scratched all over, smeared with blood.

"You don look so . . . good yerself," he mumbled.

"Tobias, there's a lot of blood on the floor, here around your head. I need to have a look at it."

"That horrible bird tried to bite off my head."

At least he could put a sentence together now.

"Yes," I said. "I see it now." The tip of the bill had sliced him something awful. I could see bone in places. "I'll be right back, Tobias. Don't move."

There came that laugh again.

I went to the cupboard and got a roll of linen, then ducked down under the table again.

"I'm going to bandage your head."

"All right."

I wrapped it tight, putting pressure on the wound. When I was finished, we sat there for a while, his head cradled in my lap. Tobias was fully awake now, and his breathing seemed easier.

"Molly?"

"Yes?"

"As charming as it is to lie under the table while you are stroking my cheek—we really must get away from here. Out of the castle, I mean, and into the town."

"I know. But I can't quite think how to do it. It's hard to be clever just now."

"Well, the first step is to get up. Then the next step is to walk down the stairs, then out the door, and into the yard."

"A brilliant plan. I never would have thought of it."

"We will make rather an eye-catching pair. Not inconspicuous."

"All the blood, you mean, and the gouges and scratches. And our ruined clothes."

"Yes. And sorry, Molly, but you reek of something dead."

"You reek, too."

I slid back, scooping his head from my lap and setting it gently on the floor. Then I crawled out from under the table.

"I'll get my other clothes. You rest. I'll be back in a minute."

I crept down the stairs and into the storeroom, where my roommates still slept. I felt my way in the darkness till I came to my little bed. Then I slipped the bundle out from under the pillow and left the room again.

No one woke.

Crouching on the floor outside the privy—near the spot where I had killed the first wolf—I unrolled the bundle and pulled out my only other clothes. They had been new when I'd worn them to the banquet, but they'd seen much hard use since, what with the prince's blood, and the river mud, and sleeping in the wet out in the open. They'd been scrubbed and mended several times, and so were reasonably clean—though shabby, very shabby, even for a scullery maid.

But they would have to do. They were all I had, and I could not go about as I was.

I changed in the privy, throwing the ruined and stinking clothes down the hole; the river would carry them away. Then I went back to the kitchen, found a cloth and some water to clean my face and hands, and returned to the pantry.

Tobias had moved out from under the table by then. He sat near the entry door, leaning against one of the silver chests.

"Ah, much better," he said when I knelt beside him. "But you might want to run your fingers through your hair. Yes. Now only one of us looks like a wounded beggar."

"How do you feel?"

"I shall live. Your head stroking seems to have cured me. You should set up shop as an apothecary."

"Ha."

I went to the far side of the room where I'd set the candlesticks on the floor. I began picking them up, two at a time, and setting them back on the table. I put them all on one end, near where Tobias sat and as far from the bowl as possible. I didn't want to look at it ever again.

But as I laid down the last of the candlesticks, I could not help but notice, out of the corner of my eye, that there was something in the bowl. Indeed, several things, rather large.

I took a candle and went over to have a look.

"Oh, Tobias!" I said. "Amazing!" I held up the prince's dagger.

He stared with astonishment. "Where did you get that? Last time I saw it, it was in the belly of a wolf."

"It came out of the bowl. And the last time I saw it, Thomas was holding it to my throat."

"Alaric's dagger?"

"Yes, the very same." I set it down on the table and reached in again, bringing out the three kitchen knives. I held them up for him to see.

His mouth still hung open; now he was speechless.

I was thinking how fortunate it was that the cook need never know that his knives had been borrowed—and certainly not what they had been used for—when I noticed something else, something small, sparkling on the bottom of the bowl. I dropped the knives and gave a little cry of delight.

"Oh!" I said. "My necklace!"

"But why is it in there? Aren't you wearing it?"

"I was, but Thomas took it from me. He thought it made me powerful and without it I was helpless." I grinned. "It appears he was wrong."

"But what do you suppose . .?" He pointed to the bowl and the knives.

"I don't know. Except that, well, these things didn't belong in there."

"So—what? The bowl just spit them out?"

"Something like that."

I thought of Thomas, then. Did he belong? I supposed he did. The bowl had been his doing. Now it would be his grave.

I put my necklace back on, tying the broken ends of the chain in a knot. Then I went into the kitchen to put away the knives. The sky was beginning to grow light. It was time for us to go.

"Can you walk, Tobias?" I asked. He was more alert now, and his color had improved.

"I may need some help. My head still swims in circles."

"All right, then, let me lift you up."

He was heavier than I thought. He slipped back down again onto the floor.

"Move that bench over beside me," he said. "I can rest one hand on it, and you can take the other. I think I can get up that way."

I led him out into the kitchen and set him to rest on a stool.

"I must tidy up," I said. "I'll be quick."

I wet a linen cloth from the pitcher of rainwater and knelt down, careful not to soil my skirts, and wiped Tobias's blood from the floor. Then I set the bench back in its place.

But what to do with the silver bowl? I longed to throw it in the river, but that seemed needless and wrong. The enchantment was broken. It would do no more harm to anyone—and it was a great treasure, a fine and beautiful thing, made by a master craftsman who just happened to be my grandfather.

And so I put it away in its accustomed place and closed the cupboard door. Then I put the other things away, too—the polishing paste, the pitcher, the linen, the candles.

"Are you ready?" I asked Tobias.

"I think so," he said. "I've been sitting upright all this time and never once tumbled to the floor."

"A good sign. Now take my arm, and we shall go get you a change of clothes. Then it's off to the hospital as soon as the gates are opened."

"Is that really necessary?"

"Perhaps not, but it's what we shall tell the guards. The hospital lies outside the walls, Tobias."

"Clever girl. So tell me then—how shall we say I got this gash on my noggin?"

"You fell down the stairs."

"Was I roaringly drunk, like poor Sebastian?"

"No. Just very, very clumsy."

We shuffled across the flagstones toward the stairway, clinging together for support, staggering comically.

"We are indeed a pitiful pair," I said.

"No—not pitiful. Wounded heroes, returned from battle."

"Why, yes, Tobias, now that you say it—I suppose that's exactly what we are."

⫷ 32 ⫸

A Stop
Along the Way

IF YOU WISH TO KNOW what goes on in the world, you have only to visit a tavern in the center of any town. If you happen to be in Westria and are interested in royal doings, you'll want to go to the Boar and Bristle.

For five days Lukas had been waiting there—drinking great bumpers of ale at the abbot's expense and listening in on others' conversations. Now he had much to tell.

It was common knowledge, he said, throughout Westria and beyond, that the prince had in fact not drowned. Now he intended to challenge Reynard for the throne, to which end he'd raised an army of supporters.

"And you'll never guess where they gathered!" Lukas widened his eyes and raised his brows to show his great amazement. "At our very own St. Bartholomew's Abbey! What do you think of that? But then, see"—he leaned forward now and gave us a knowing wink—"I'm thinking perhaps you knew sommat of this afore. And your visit to the castle, that was some sort of important, secret business. Ain't that so?"

"You may be right," I said.

He beamed with satisfaction.

"They've left the abbey now, on their way here. And every village they pass, more people join 'em. 'Tis a ragtag army they say, nothing but farmers, and cobblers, and beggars, and such. A few small landholding gents."

"He has some knights, surely," Tobias said. "And gentlemen of high rank."

"Oh, aye. But not so many as you could take a castle with. And speaking of that—Reynard's bringing in men by the score, and wagonloads of provisions. They're getting ready for a siege, they are."

"We know that too," I said. "Have you heard where Alaric is now?"

"A good day's ride from here. They move slow,

what with so many; and they must provision 'em all."

"Will you take us there?"

"Aye, if you want. But there's no need. Just wait right here, and he'll come to you."

"We can't wait. We have news for the prince, and he'll want to hear it as soon as possible."

"Then I'm off to the stables this very minute. You tell the waiter we'll need food for the road—bread, cheese, ale, and such. Then I'll pay the bill, and we'll be on our way."

"Good," I said. "Make haste."

"Don't you worry, miss. Big doin's, ain't it?" And he hurried off, chuckling to himself.

⁂

Lukas drove the cart rather faster than was needful—or comfortable, for that matter, after a night of battling curses. Tobias had been to see a barber-surgeon who had stitched up his head proper and put a clean bandage on it. But Tobias said it still throbbed most awfully, especially when we hit a rut or a bump, which we did right often.

We were well away from the town now, at a point where the road skirted the king's hunting preserve. It was a pleasant spot, with the land sloping down toward the river on one side and the wooded park on the other, bare trees casting shadows on the new-fallen snow.

"Tobias," I said, "are we anywhere near the place where Mary is buried?"

He turned to me, surprised. "Yes," he said.

"Did you mark the grave? With a cross or a stone?"

"A stone."

"Do you think you could find it again? Would you like to go there?"

"You can read my very thoughts."

"It wasn't so hard, Tobias. Have we passed the place already?"

"No, it's a bit farther on. There was a farmhouse on the left side of the road. We cut off into the woods so as not to be seen. There was a big, old, gnarly tree. I'll know it when I see it."

Not long after we came to the tree, and I called for Lukas to stop, saying he should rest the horses and have himself sommat to eat. We'd be back shortly. He raised his eyebrows and grinned. He thought we were off on more important business.

But then, that was true. We were.

Tobias made his way through the woods as though treading a well-remembered path. "There is the pine," he said, pointing, "and the outcropping of granite. I picked a poor place to dig a grave." He gave a snort of bitter laughter. "Rocks, nothing but rocks."

"You were just a boy."

"I was. But I thought myself a man."

"Well, you cared for your family as a man would do. Better than most."

A few more steps up the rising ground and Tobias stopped, and squatted, and swept the snow off a large stone. Then he cleared the area beside it and laid his hand upon the grave.

"This is the place," he said.

"It's lovely, Tobias. Perfect."

He nodded.

"Hello, Mary," I said, touching the grave too. "I'm Molly. Tobias tells me you're fond of kissing elbows."

Tobias closed his eyes.

Too much, I thought. *Best not to say any more.* I got up and wandered away, looking around me at the silent woods. It was indeed a fine place to bury a child. There would be friendly forest creatures about— birds, deer, chipmunks, foxes, squirrels. They would keep her company through the long days. And in the wintertime, like now, when the leaves had all fallen from the trees, she could look up at night and see the stars.

An idea came to me then, and I began to search for a branch that was straight and strong. I snapped one off a tree and carried it back to the grave. Tobias looked up and smiled; his face was wet with tears.

"May I give her a gift?" I asked.

He shrugged. "Of course. Why not?"

I wiped more snow away until I found a rock of such a size as would fit neatly in my hand. Then just behind Mary's gravestone I hammered the stick into the ground. It took a while; the earth was winter-hard. But the branch had a point to it where I'd broken it off the tree, and it bit into the soil. I gathered a few more stones and piled them around the base of the stick to make sure it stayed in place.

Tobias watched me curiously.

"Are you making a cross?" he finally asked.

"No," I said. Then I pulled the ribbons out of my apron pocket. "They're a bit rumpled and not so clean as they were when first you gave them to me, but I think she'll like them all the same."

I tied the ribbons to the top of the stick, with a knot in the middle of each, the four tails hanging down.

"It's as merry as a Maypole," Tobias said.

"Yes, that's what I thought. In the summer the breezes will blow them very charmingly; and that will delight her, don't you think?"

"Oh, it will. I'm sure of it."

"And it's a gift from both of us, so she'll like it all the more."

"You're a good soul, Molly," he said.

We both wept a little, there in the woods. Then we followed our tracks back to the road, and Lukas, and the cart.

⚜ 33 ⚜

The Encampment

IT WAS LATE BY THE TIME we reached the encampment.

For miles we kept thinking we were almost there, for all about us were the prince's followers—gathered around campfires, huddling under makeshift tents. They lined the road and spread out onto the frozen fields on either side.

"There are so many," Tobias said.

"Aye," Lukas grumbled. "An army of unwashed peasants. Good for nothing but to slow him down."

I suspected that was true. But all the same it tugged at my heart, the love these people felt for their prince, that they would leave the grim comfort of their homes in wintertime to follow him and fight for him however they could.

The moon was high above the hills by the time we reached the edge of the encampment. The road was guarded by a handful of gangly boys, knights in training most like. They called us to halt and asked what our business was—had we come to join the prince as the others had? For if so, there was no room in the village.

"We're here on important business," Lukas said pompously. "This here cart, I'll have you know, belongs to the Abbot Elias. And I am in his employ."

"The abbot is housed just a ways down the road. Third cottage on your left. But it's full. You cannot stay there."

"So you say. But we ain't here to see the abbot just now. We've come special to speak with the prince himself."

"That is not possible," said the boy.

"Well now, see, I think it is. Because these two young people here"—he pointed in our direction—"have only just returned from a secret mission."

"Lukas!" Tobias said, then to the boy, "Just tell us where the prince is staying, and we'll speak to his bodyguards ourselves. Let them decide if we may see him or no."

"As you will. He's in the largest cottage, just round the bend on your right. But he won't see you."

The cottage was well guarded, by real soldiers. No beardless boys this time.

"Who goes there?" one of them wanted to know.

"Friends of the prince," I said, "and I assure you he will be glad to hear the news we bring."

There was mocking laughter. "I'm sure of it," someone said.

"Ask him, then, will he see Molly and Tobias? If you send us away and he finds out, I promise you shall regret it."

The guard stepped forward and squinted at me, the corners of his mouth curling up a little. He didn't know what to make of us.

"What have you come about?"

"Alaric's business, which he sent us on."

The guard stepped away and conferred with the others in whispered voices. They were quite under-standably reluctant to bother the prince at such an hour. And we didn't look like the sort of people who would be sent on an important mission. Still—what if we really did carry important news?

Finally one of them knocked three times, then opened the door and went in.

"You wait right where you are," another guard said. "Don't you move or we shall have to—"

Just then the door was opened by Alaric himself.

"Molly! Tobias! Come in and tell me all. Aren't you cold? Oh, it's such a night! Come in, come in!"

The soldiers stepped aside. I wrinkled my nose at them as we passed by.

Alaric sat us down, then picked up a pitcher of ale. He carried it over to the fire, pulled a poker out of the coals, and plunged it hissing into the brew. Then he came back and poured us each a cup of warm ale. It was village made, no better than Margaret's, yet he offered it with a smile and even took some himself.

"So, you lived to tell the tale," he said. His eyes were bright with feverish excitement. "Oh, I rejoice at it, truly. Roger!" he called to his valet. "Run tell the kitchen girl to cook us up some sausages. We'll have some bread and mustard to go with it. Say she's to bring it out herself, if she would."

Then he turned back to us and flashed another dazzling smile—all eagerness, and satisfaction, and isn't-it-fine-to-be-me? Truly, it was something to behold. He shimmered like the very sun.

"You seem well, my lord," said Tobias, stating the obvious. "And we likewise rejoice—"

"Yes," he said, and the sun disappeared behind a cloud. "But I believe you have something to tell me. I would hear it now."

"My lord," I said, "you may be at peace. The bowl can do no more harm."

"It is destroyed, then?"

"No, sire. It's as perfect and beautiful as ever it was. But the evil that lived in its heart is gone. When you get to the castle, you can do with it as you will."

He looked at me and then at Tobias, his expression very grave. "You've been injured," he said, touching his own head in the spot where Tobias wore his bandage. Then to me: "You're wounded, too."

"There was a bit of a scuffle," I said. "We'll mend."

"A bit of a scuffle, eh? I begin to think there is nothing you cannot manage, little Molly."

"I hardly think that is true."

"Well, I say it is. Must you always contradict me? Can you not just say 'thank you?'"

We were both of us grinning.

"Thank you, my lord."

Tobias took a drink of ale and gazed down at his knees. Finally he cleared his throat and said, "There is something else you must know, Your Majesty. It's very important."

"Tell me, then."

"It's not Reynard who is your enemy."

"But surely—"

"It's Gertrude, sire."

"Gertrude? You are speaking of my aunt? She's an old woman."

"Yes, my lord. Molly, tell him."

"Well, sire, long ago when she was about my age, her father was without a son to inherit the throne."

"I know all this."

"But that was the source of her grievance, you see— that she could not be the heir, though she was the king's only child, just because she was a girl. Then, of course, she was married off to the crown prince of Austlind—"

"Osgood, yes, I know. And when Mortimer finally despaired of a son, he offered the throne to Osgood, only to withdraw the offer altogether after my father was born. It was clumsy, and I do not doubt that it stung, for Gertrude is proud. But it's the common way of things. Thrones pass from father to son."

"That may be, lord prince, yet Gertrude *did* resent it, and she *was* angry—enough to cast a malediction on her own family."

"You're telling me that she went to the silversmith and asked him to make her a bowl that would curse the newborn prince?"

"No. She couldn't do it herself. But she had a noble servant who had come with her from Westria. He loved her very much and believed her cause was righteous. He gave her his pledge to do whatever she asked of him. It was he who commissioned the bowl, my lord—and murdered the silversmith, too."

"Your grandfather."

"Yes."

"How do you know all this?"

"Some of it I saw in a vision. Thomas told me the rest."

"Thomas? The keeper of the silver?"

"Yes, my lord. He was the noble servant."

"No! I cannot believe it."

"Nor could I. But he murdered your family, Alaric. And he wished you dead as well. He told me so just before he tried to kill me."

I nodded at Tobias. He pulled out the prince's dagger and laid it on the table. Alaric took it up and studied it for a time, turning it in his hands, running his finger along the flat of the blade.

"Where did you get this?" he said. "I never thought to see it again."

"Thomas had it. He held it to my throat." I pulled down the top of my bodice, just enough to show him the gash.

"He did that?"

"Yes. But he's dead now."

"You killed him?"

"No. But I watched him die."

Alaric sighed. His mind was already moving on to something else. "How am I to challenge a frail old woman who was sister to my own father?"

"I cannot say, my lord. It's a bit of a problem, all right."

He slid down in his chair, his hands draped at his side, legs akimbo, and stared up at the ceiling.

"I think you must go through Reynard," Tobias suggested. But the rest of what he said I did not hear, for my attention strayed elsewhere. The prince had not changed from his traveling clothes, you see. He still had on his boots and his hooded cape, which was fastened at the neck with—

"My lord!" I cried, interrupting Tobias. "Your brooch! Had you another one just like it or—?"

He looked at me and smiled, just as gaily as before. Then he turned and roared toward the back of the house: "Where *is* that kitchen wench?"

He was so changeful this night—bright, then dark,

from one moment to the next. You never knew which Alaric it was going to be.

"Sausages just ready now" came a voice from the next room. "Here we are, milord, with a nice hunk of bread, like you asked for, and a wee pot of mus—" She spied us then, and screamed, and nearly dropped the tray. "Molls! Oh, my sainted eyeballs!"

I gasped, and Tobias gaped, and Alaric howled with laughter.

"Winifred!" I cried. "I cannot believe it. How came you to be here?"

"Oh, oh, oh!" she moaned, patting her bosom and breathing hard, trying to recover from the surprise. "Well, I did manage to find me a place in the house of a nobleman in our parts. And then he was called up by the prince. And so I went to him, secretlike, and told him what we had done to save Alaric from the wolves, you know, and how my mother had been his wisewoman and all. I begged leave to come join the prince, and he allowed it. I brought his brooch back," she added with pride, "which we'd been keeping safe for him. And don't he look fine now, all mended and walking around like a normal person?"

We agreed he most definitely did.

"All right. That's enough, ladies." Alaric was all

business again. "You may chatter all you like in the morning. But now we must finish our talk. It's late, and I've been traveling all day. Winifred, thank you for the sausages. I'll call you to come for the tray as soon as we're done."

She gave us a wink, then curtsied, and backed out of the room.

The prince cut a slice of the dark village bread and slathered it with mustard. Then he speared a sausage with his knife, and wrapped the bread around it, and took a hearty bite. We watched him chew, then swallow.

"Go ahead," he urged between bites, "try a sausage. They're surprisingly edible."

I grinned. "You've developed a taste for peasant fare?"

"Not in the least. But I've had little else since I left the castle, and one . . . accommodates, does one not?"

I supposed one did, if one knew what *accommodate* meant. As I did not, I merely shrugged. "Now," he said. "What more have you to tell?"

"Only that Reynard is preparing for a siege," Tobias said. "But I suspect you know that already."

"Yes. Everyone knows it."

"Then there's nothing more, really. I think we ought to go and leave you to your rest."

"No, stay a moment longer. Roger, run over to Brother Eutropious. If he's asleep, wake him up. Ask if he has space for my two friends here. Say I wish him to tend to their wounds as tenderly as he once did to mine."

"Yes, Your Highness."

"Brother Eutropious!" Tobias said as soon as Roger was gone. "He is with you also? Is all the world here?"

"It does seem that way, does it not? Yes, Eutropious *would* come, *would* not be dissuaded, for he trusts no one else to look after my shoulder, though truly it is almost healed. Now before you go, there is something I seem to have forgotten."

"What is that?" I asked.

"I have not thanked you yet." He wiped mustard off his hands and cheeks with a linen napkin, then laid it on the table and addressed us in earnest. "And I cannot do it handsomely enough. For the curse that has plagued my family since the time of my father's birth and robbed me most cruelly of my parents, and my brothers, and my poor, dear sister shall cast its shadow over me no longer."

His voice broke as he said it, and he turned his head aside, as there were tears welling in his eyes and he probably thought it unmanly to weep. When he had mastered himself, he went on.

"I need no longer fear for myself, nor for any sons and daughters God may grant me in the future. My destiny rests in my own hands now, as it should—all because of you."

"It was an honor," I said.

"I know you haven't told me everything, how you risked your lives in that 'bit of a scuffle.' It seems there is no end to what you are willing to do in my service, and in the service of the kingdom. I also understand that you did not do it for gain, but as soon as I am able—if I am able—I shall reward you as richly as you deserve. You shall have land, and wealth, and titles, and anything else you should desire."

I watched him closely as he said all this and saw a new expression on his face, a different kind of smile than I had seen before. There was real affection in that grin, such as you might show to an equal, to a friend, to someone you deeply cared for. And I felt my heart swell with love for him. Oh, he would make such a fine king! A fire was burning inside of him now, a passion and a purpose. In just a few months he had grown from a boy to a man—and he looked to be a great one, too. Like the thousands of humble folk camped all round the village that frosty night, I would gladly have followed him anywhere.

Alaric reached out and offered a hand to each of us.

"I have one more favor to ask. I wish you to ride at my side tomorrow. You are my good-luck charm, Molly. No harm can ever come to me when you are near."

"Oh, my lord," I said. "I would be most honored to do it, but I never sat upon a horse in my life. I fear I would fall off and be trampled. At the very least I would cause your knights to laugh themselves into convulsions."

"Then I shall ride beside your cart," he said, and chuckled at the thought of it.

The door opened then, and Roger came in.

"Brother Eutropious says he would be most glad to tend to the young people and that he will find them some spot to sleep—though he is not sure where exactly, as it is already very crowded in there. He will put up the driver as well."

"Excellent. Go with them, if you will. Show them the place."

Roger nodded, and we got up to leave.

"But first, Molly—"

"Yes, my lord?"

"I would have a private word with you."

❦ 34 ❧

An Army
of Innocents

WE WAITED ON THE RISE that overlooked the castle from the west. Below us the land sloped down, past winter-fallow fields, and the huts of sharecroppers, and on to Castleton—where Tobias had been born and watched his family die—and beyond that to the castle itself, and to the river that protected it from the east. Swarming across those fields, and streaming through the villages and the town, were thousands and thousands of Alaric's followers.

They were peasants mostly, and shopkeepers, and artisans. Except for the knights and noblemen who stayed close by the prince to protect him, none of these people were trained in war. Nor were they equipped in the common way of armies, though a few did carry swords. The rest made do with whatever they had: scythes, and pitchforks, and pruning hooks, and homemade lances. There were women among them too—children even, some of them carrying little flags they had made out of sticks and handkerchiefs.

Oh, Alaric, I thought, *I hope you know what you're doing.* For up on the ramparts of that great, impregnable castle were two dozen archers at least, ready with their longbows to send a rain of arrows down upon those innocents.

It was hard not to mention this to the prince.

"Will there be a battle, my lord?"

"No, I think not."

"Then why are we here?"

"You shall see," he said. "Now, Molly, I very much wish you to be with me to the end of this journey. You are my good-luck charm, remember? But the cart, I'm afraid, will utterly spoil the effect. Tobias, can you sit a horse?"

"If it isn't leaping over hedgerows, my lord."

"Excellent. Roger, see if you can find us a proper

mount—something gentle and strong. Then I believe we are ready to begin."

"But what about Molly, sire?" Tobias asked.

"She shall ride behind you."

I didn't say a word.

In time a large gray mare was brought forward, and Tobias climbed up into the saddle. Then he took his foot out from one of the stirrups, and I was bid to put mine into it—at which point several of the prince's men heaved me upward and shouted, all at the same time, that I must swing my other leg over the horse, which I did. And then there I was, on the animal's soft and slippery rump, clutching fiercely to Tobias.

"Nicely done," Alaric said. "Now stay by my side."

And down the hill we went, with trumpets blaring and flags flying, flanked by Alaric's royal guard: lords great and small with their knights and other vassals.

When the crowd saw we were on the move, they parted to let us through—cheering themselves hoarse, reaching out to touch the very air the prince passed through. Women held their babies up to catch a glimpse of him. Children leaped up and down, squealing and waving their little flags. Wizened farmers raised their pruning hooks and shouted brave hurrahs.

I began to understand what Alaric had in mind, what he'd meant by a "moral victory." For at that moment we were all as one, united in a common cause, from the lowest cropper to the greatest noble. *We* were the kingdom of Westria and Alaric our rightful king. Surely Reynard, gazing down at the spectacle from the ramparts, must have felt a worm in his belly—like a boy who'd been caught stealing sweets.

We came to a halt near the castle walls, within shouting distance. Now the crowd was urged to fall back, to open a space for what would come next.

Alaric dismounted and stepped forward—alone and vulnerable in his borrowed, travel-worn clothes, his yellow hair blowing in the wind. He wore no armor, and he'd waved his guards away. A single arrow would have done for him, and this would all be over.

Oh, you have plentiful courage, my dearest prince. But are you wise? I bit my lip and waited. I think everyone did the same. The crowd was remarkably quiet.

Up on the ramparts, in addition to the archers, there stood a crowd of people—some of Reynard's knights, no doubt, along with other noble supporters and probably his three proud sons, glad of some excitement. There were women among them, too; I could see the gay colors of their gowns, though I could not tell who any of them were.

But surely, *surely* Gertrude was among them. She would not miss this for the world.

Reynard leaned over the wall now, looking down at us. He wore a breastplate but no helmet. I thought I saw contempt upon his face. Or was it amusement?

Alaric gave a signal, and a trumpet sounded.

"Cousin!" he shouted. "I come in peace, for I know you to be a fair man. You assumed the throne believing me dead; and there is nothing improper in what you did, for you are indeed next in the line of succession. But as you can see, I am very much alive. And so I come now to declare myself, to you and to all these people here assembled, the rightful heir to the throne of Westria."

"Cousin!" came Reynard's booming reply. "What charming soldiers you have, armed with sticks and pitchforks. I wonder if my archers have sufficient arrows to dispatch them all. I believe they do, though I think they will not need them; your mighty force of peasants will trample one another as they run away."

Alaric had not expected this. "You do not acknowledge me then, cousin?"

"I acknowledge that you are my cousin. Will that do?" And he laughed at his own wit.

Alaric stood speechless, his hair blowing, his eyes squinting into the sun.

"This is not going well," I whispered to Tobias.

"No," he agreed.

"You must help me down, and quickly."

"Why?"

"There's something I need to say to the prince."

"Now, Molly? This isn't a good time."

"It's the absolute perfect time. How do I get off this blasted horse?"

"Well, you put your foot in the stirrup, and do what you did before—only backward. Grip my hand. Yes, just so."

"Excuse me! Excuse me!" I pushed my way through the crowd till I came to the edge. "Alaric!" I called. "There is something I must tell you."

He looked at me uncomprehendingly, astonished that I would interrupt him at such a moment.

"You need to hear it," I said.

And so the prince held up his hand to Reynard— *Wait a moment, I shall be back*—and walked over to me. "It had better be important," he said.

"This is just like our little scuffle," I said. "We

were outnumbered; the odds were overwhelming. But the Guardian knew every one of those dreadful creatures, had known them since they were infants. He told me which were slow, and which were stupid, and which were vain. And so we used their weak points against them and won. Alaric, what do you know about Reynard?"

"I told you before. He's lazy. He likes things easy. Truly, I am surprised to see him so bold today."

"But this *is* easy. He has the castle packed with knights, and you have an army of peasants. That's why he's laughing. He need do nothing much, and it's all his."

"This isn't helping me, Molly." Alaric was about to leave. I grabbed his arm and stopped him.

"Alaric—is he brave?"

"Not particularly. No."

"Good. For this will help you, I promise. Reynard does not know that the curses in the bowl have been destroyed. No one knows but the three of us."

"Does he know about the bowl at all?"

"I doubt it. But his mother does."

"So? I don't understand you, Molly." Alaric was at the edge of his patience now.

"Alaric, the bowl cursed the royal house of Westria—and no one else."

He stared at me, his mind working for a precious long time, while the crowd began to grow restless. Then he finally understood and broke into one of those dazzling smiles.

"You *are* my good-luck charm," he said.

❦ 35 ❧

A Moral Victory

"CONSULTING WITH YOUR GENERAL there, cousin?"

"You are as witty as ever, Reynard. And braver than I thought you to be. For I should not have believed—with a kingdom of your own, and a handsome castle there in Austlind with such a lovely view of the mountains, and all your many estates with their fine deer parks, and jousting grounds, and ponds, and rose gardens, and orchards—that you would risk your life to get Westria, too."

"Risk my life? You think I fear that rabble?"

"I don't refer to these good countryfolk. I am speaking of the curse, Reynard, that has long plagued the house of Westria. If you become king and I am disinherited, it will be your blood it seeks, and that of your family—not mine."

"You think to scare me with fireside tales?"

"You were there when the wolves came, Reynard, and my brother died—and my mother, God rest her soul, and my poor sister."

"Yes. I was there."

"Did they harm you? Or your mother? Your sons? Or anyone else for that matter, besides my family?"

"That was mere chance. You survived, I notice."

"But I, too, was singled out from all the others. I was attacked and sorely wounded. Had it not been for friends who came to my aid, you would have inherited Westria honestly. And so I ask you again: is that what you wish—to look over your shoulder for the rest of your life? To see your sons buried before their time, struck down in peculiar ways? For that is what it means to rule Westria."

"I don't believe your fanciful tales," he said. "You read too many storybooks."

"Then ask your mother. Ask Gertrude."

"Nonsense, Alaric. I've heard enough. Leave this place now, and take your people with you, or I shall unleash my bowmen. And be assured, you shall have the first arrow."

"*Ask your mother*, Reynard! Ask her about the silver

bowl, the fine gift she sent on the occasion of my father's birth. Ask about the silversmith who made it, and what he put into it—besides silver. You might also tell her that Thomas will not be around to do her bidding anymore; but before he died he admitted what he'd done. I think once you have heard what Gertrude has to say, you will not be so eager to take my kingdom anymore. Go ahead. What harm can it do?"

I held my breath as a figure broke away from the crowd and came up to Reynard, a woman dressed in a plum-colored gown. She wore a linen headdress, so I could not see if she was white haired or dark. But I knew who it was.

Reynard turned to her, and they spoke. She touched his arm. He leaned forward, then pulled suddenly away. He seemed angry and unsure what to do.

"Was that your idea?" Tobias asked me.

"Yes," I said.

"Shrewd."

"I know, wasn't it?"

Reynard was back at the wall again calling to Alaric. "Cousin!" he said. "I find we have done you a terrible wrong, you and all your kin. I knew nothing of it."

"That is true!" Alaric said to the people around him.

"But tell me—are you not afraid of this curse?"

"I've lived with it all my life, and watched my family die one by one. But it's my duty, and my heritage. As to why you should wish to take it on, I cannot imagine. There is little to gain and a great price to pay. So what will it be, Reynard? Will you signal your archers and take my life right here before the walls of Dethemere Castle? Or will you acknowledge me, and open the gates, then pack your belongings and go home—to live out your life in comfort and prosperity, and watch your boys grow to manhood and your mother die a natural death in her bed—though the saints know she does not deserve it. What shall it be, Reynard?"

The crowd, which had been listening in stunned amazement, now let forth a hearty roar. "Go home!" they cried. "Go home! Go home!"

Reynard signaled to one of his knights, and then a second one; they escorted Gertrude away. He watched her go, then returned to the wall. He looked out at the hushed and anxious crowd that filled the valley as far as eye could see.

"I won't have my mother answering for what she did," he said. "She is old and she believed most truly that she was wronged. But I will take her home with me and lock her in her chamber, under guard night and day. She shall never leave that room until the moment of her death. Will that satisfy you?"

"Yes. There's been enough royal blood spilled already."

"Good. Archers, stand down. Let the gates be opened. Come into your castle, young Alaric, and rule your country well. I acknowledge you as king of Westria."

❦ 36 ❧

A Private
Conversation

"**THAT NIGHT AT THE PRINCE'S** encampment, when he asked for a private word . . ."

"Yes, Tobias?"

"You were there a long time—while we waited out in the cold."

"I'm sorry. He had something important to ask me."

"Words he couldn't say in my hearing?"

"It was of a personal nature."

"Oh, I see."

"*Do* you, Tobias? *Really*?"

"I can guess."

"Go ahead then."

Silence.

"All right. Had it something to do with marriage?"

"Mmmmm . . . yes. It did."

"*His* marriage?"

"Yes again. Isn't this fun?"

"Do I look like I'm enjoying it?"

"No. But you're getting warm."

"All right then, here's what I think: I believe you love Alaric. I believe you've loved him since that day you first saw him in the hall, when you threatened to stick him and stuff him—"

"I never threatened. I only meant—"

"But you love him?"

"Of course I do."

"And he loves you?"

"Well he must, for I have done him a very great service. And he also thinks I bring him good luck. And I make him laugh."

"True enough."

"And likewise he loves you, Tobias, for you served him just as I did."

"Oh for heaven's sake, Molly, must you torture me so?"

"Do I—torture you?"

"Yes, of course you do! You squeeze my heart. You—"

"Good!"

"Molly, whatever has come over you?"

"I wasn't sure I could—squeeze your heart, that is."

"Well you can. I'm glad it pleases you."

I waited.

"So Alaric wishes to marry?"

"Yes, he does. He thinks it is wise not to wait very long. He must have an heir."

"And that is what he discussed with you in private."

"We do keep returning to that. Yes it was."

"Molly—does Alaric wish to marry *you*?"

And then I laughed so hard, I nearly lost my breakfast. And when I finally got control of myself, I lost it again and laughed harder still. My face grew hot, and tears streamed down my cheeks. I was gasping for breath.

"Are you done?"

"I'm not sure. I hope so. For truly if I laugh anymore, I shall be sick all over this beautiful gown."

"I think you've had fun enough at my expense—"

"Yes, Tobias. And you bore it like a saint. So I shall be plain now and not torture you any longer. Alaric would never wed a scullion, not even one who brings him luck and has risked her life in his service—not even after she has been raised to great estate, as you and I have been."

"I see."

"Tobias—he wishes to marry *the princess from Cortova*. Surely you remember—the dark beauty who was meant to marry Edmund? But she left under rather awkward circumstances, and he wishes to be sure of her before he asks. He is proud and could not bear to be refused. And so he wondered whether my family, by any chance, still had one of Grandfather's Loving Cups."

"Do they?"

"Of course not."

"Was he disappointed?"

"Rather. But he got over it somewhat when I gave him my necklace. I explained that the silver was full of happy magic, just like a Loving Cup. He was a bit worried that there were already initials on it, and they were neither his nor hers. He thought perhaps he could get it altered, have a silversmith turn the *W* and the *M* into vines and curlicues so they'd blend in with the rest of the design. And, of course, he'd need to get a new chain."

"I am astonished."

"That I gave him my necklace?"

"Yes. It always protected you."

"I used to think so."

"It has no . . . special powers, then?"

"Oh, it does. That's why I gave it to Alaric. He wore it on the day he challenged Reynard. Here"—I touched my chest—"beneath his doublet. I think it gave him courage, made him feel invincible. It wouldn't have stopped an arrow, though."

"But why give it away, Molly—even to the prince?"

"When I left home all those years ago, my mother gave me that necklace. I asked her the same question: Why give it to me? Why not keep it for yourself?"

"And?"

"She thought it would protect and comfort me, and she expected my life would be hard—what with hearing voices and seeing visions and all. But I never really needed it, and neither did she. Uncle taught me that—and Thomas, too, when he took my necklace. I was the same without it. The power lies within *me*, Tobias. It's in my blood."

"You're magical then?"

"Do I seem so?"

"Yes. You always have."

"Well, then. There you are."

"Did Alaric remember to thank you, I wonder?"

Silence.

"Molly?"

"He is who he is, Tobias, and I shall hear nothing said against him."

"Ah."

"There's one more thing. Alaric was glad to have the necklace, but his mind was still fixed on the cup. So he wondered, you know, about my family—whether there might not be a few of them left back in the town where Grandfather lived. He thought that perhaps one of *them* might still have a Loving Cup from the old days. And if not, well, perhaps one might be found in a pawnshop in that town. Or wasn't it possible that some magical cousin had carried on the family tradition and gone into the silversmithing line . . ."

"And might be persuaded to make one for the king of Westria."

"Yes. So he asked whether I wasn't just a little curious to meet those relatives, assuming they exist, of course."

"And?"

"Well, of course I am. And as we are rich now, and have no work to do, we might as well have ourselves an adventure—and if we should happen to find Alaric a Loving Cup, so much the better."

"*We,* Molly? You're that sure of me, then?"

"As sure as I am that the sun will rise in the east and that winter will be followed by spring."

"Then I will go with you. And if we should be so fortunate as to find *two* Loving Cups, I shall buy one for myself—as I am rich now and have nothing to spend my money on."

"Oh, Tobias," I said.

"What, Molly?"

"*You* don't need one."

MOLLY'S ADVENTURES CONTINUE IN

The
Cup and the
Crown

❦ 1 ❧

King Alaric the Younger

THE GREAT HALL WAS MUCH as she remembered it: the tapestries, the massive iron candle stands, the enormous fireplace, the great gilt screen behind the dais. But the rushes were gone from the floor now, in keeping with the latest fashion. And there were sentries posted at the entrance to the royal chambers. They followed her with their eyes as she paced in restless circles, waiting. What was taking Alaric so long?

There had never been guards in the old days, when Godfrey the Lame was king. Molly knew this for a fact. She'd once pressed her ear to that very door and listened to young Prince Alaric quarreling with his mother, unobserved by anyone but Tobias, who'd come to mend the fire. He'd been scandalized that a scullery maid should presume to eavesdrop on a queen.

Molly smiled, remembering how intensely she'd despised them both. "Mind who you look at, wench," Prince Alaric had said to her as he stormed out of his mother's room. And "You aren't fit to be here," Tobias had added later. What *she'd* said didn't bear repeating—but then she'd only been seven at the time, and inclined to say whatever popped into her head, however outrageous it might be.

Come to think of it, that last part hadn't changed so very much.

She circled past the dais and was musing on the screen when the door flew open and a large, imposing man came out, thunder on his face, his boots striking the flagstones with the force of his anger. As he passed, he shot Molly a look of pure revulsion. Then he turned away, as from something loathsome, and continued with long strides down the length of that cavernous room, the stink of his fury trailing behind. She watched him, appalled, till he was long out of sight. Only when she heard her name did she look back at the door and see Alaric standing there.

He didn't greet her with a smile or apologize for making her wait. Indeed, he scarcely looked at her at all.

"Come," he said. "We'll walk in the garden. I need a change of air."

❧ ❧

He took her arm and held it close to his side. Whether he did this out of affection or was merely stiff with rage, Molly couldn't tell. Either way, she liked it. She cast a quick glance up at his pale, narrow face, his sun-bright curls and gray eyes, and judged him as handsome as ever—despite the scowl and the crease between his brows. She sighed to herself in quiet satisfaction and leaned her head against his shoulder, just a touch.

It was high summer, and the flower beds were bright with lilacs, roses, and lilies. Ancient trees arched over their heads, offering welcome shade as they followed their winding course, fine gravel crunching beneath their feet.

Molly had never been there before, though she'd lived half her life at Dethemere Castle. Common servants had no business in the king's garden, unless it was to plant, and prune, and tend that private little patch of paradise. Her place had been in the kitchen, scrubbing pots and polishing silver.

All that had changed this past half year. And nothing about her transformation from scullion to lady had struck her quite so forcibly as this: that she walked the paths of the royal garden on the arm of the king of Westria—just the two of them, alone.

Never mind that he was in a mood.

"So, how do you like your new estate?" He said this distractedly, his mind on something else.

"It's very beautiful, my lord."

"I should certainly hope so. It was to have been my sister's dower house. You're happy there?"

"Not especially, my lord."

He stopped and looked down at her, *really* looked for the first time that morning.

"*'Not especially*, my lord'?"

"It's too grand for me, Alaric. I don't belong. And those highborn servants, brought in to attend a princess, being asked to serve the likes of me . . ."

"You're a lady now, by royal decree."

"Yes. And you could royally decree that henceforth eels shall fly and magpies shall swim in the sea. But even *you* have not the power to make it so. My ladies of the chamber certainly know what I am. They correct my manners at table and express amazement that I can't do embroidery, or play the lute, or dance, or read romances. And there's nothing for me to do all day but meet with my steward and my chamberlain to talk about things I don't understand, and choose which gown to wear, and sit staring into the fire or out the window while my ladies drive me mad with their never-ending chatter."

"Merciful heavens! You're *bored* as well?"

"Unbearably."

She could feel the tension in his body. He held her arm in a viselike grip.

"Any minute now you're going to say that you're awfully sorry, you know you've been shockingly rude, but it's all because you were ill raised."

"I suppose that would be—"

"Well, *a plague* on your upbringing! I'm sick of hearing about it. I can see you now in your dotage." He took the high, nasal voice of an old crone, hunching his back for added effect. "Oh, I'm *so* sorry I insulted you, my lord, but when I was a small child—*fifty years* ago—I was not taught how to behave."

She took a deep breath. "Your Majesty," she said, "I truly *am* sorry that I seem so ungrateful when you have been so generous and kind. But I spoke the truth: I don't have the makings of a lady. You'd have done better to set me up as a shopkeeper—"

"If you say another word, I shall bite off your head."

How was it, she wondered as they continued to walk in stormy silence, that she'd been so careful of what she said to the cook when she'd worked in the palace kitchens and cowered under the haughty gazes of her ladies of the chamber—yet with the *king of Westria,* well, she'd say just *any* old thing!

"I'll find you some better attendants," he muttered, "and see that they treat you with respect."

When she didn't respond, he added, "You may speak now."

"Thank you, my lord, but you can leave them as they are. In the end I found it rather amusing to torture them."

"*Torture* them? Good God!"

"Not with thumbscrews, never fear. I just developed a sudden fondness for exercise—taking long walks to the village or the next town over, in foul weather whenever possible. And as I cannot go out alone, it being unfitting for a lady—"

"—they have to accompany you."

"Yes. Such a lot of mud this year."

She'd finally made him laugh. And it felt for a brief spell like the old times, before he'd become king and the burden of great responsibility had been laid on his young shoulders, along with his royal robes.

"Alaric," she said softly. "Tell me why I'm here." She already knew, of course. She'd known for weeks, long before the royal messenger had arrived at Barcliffe Manor, calling her back to court. She knew because she'd seen it in a vision.

The first time it had happened, she'd taken it for a dream. But it had been too clear, too perfect; and when she'd sat up in bed. it had stayed with her, not fading away like smoke into air as dreams always do. It had returned the following night, and every night thereafter, always exactly the same: a handsome boy of eighteen or twenty, dressed in fine clothes, holding a beautiful goblet. And though she'd never seen the cup before, she knew exactly what it was—and what it meant for her, and for the king.

As for the boy, he was a mystery.

"I want you to go to Austlind," Alaric said, "to find one of your grandfather's Loving Cups."

"I thought that must be it," she said. "You were so keen to have one last winter—then not another word. I kept expecting . . . but I suppose you've had a lot on your mind these past months."

"Learning to be a king, you mean? And taking control of my country, and choosing my counselors, and fending off officious busybodies who say I'm too young to rule and I must have a regent do it for me?"

"Yes. And I suppose that terrible man who came out of your chambers just now is one of the busybodies?"

"Lord Mayhew? Oh, yes. You know what he calls

me behind my back? King Alaric the Younger. Isn't that charming?"

"You should chop off his head."

"Oh, please, Molly, be serious. I'm sending him with you to Austlind, by the way, to see to your safety on the road. That's why he was so angry. He feels the mission is beneath him."

"Then why send him? If he mocks you in secret, surely he cannot be trusted."

"I trust him to keep you safe. As for the rest, I just told him you're going to Austlind to find a certain silver cup, which I want to send as a gift to the king of Cortova. Anything regarding the princess or the special properties of the cup—please keep that to yourself."

They'd reached an opening in the boxwood hedge that led to the heart of the garden. Here was a pond with a stone fish rising out of the center, standing upright on its tail, water spouting from its mouth.

They sat on a long stone bench in the shade of a chestnut tree. The king released her arm.

"Now, in addition to Lord Mayhew, I'm sending my valet. His name is Stephen, he's fluent in the language of Austlind, and he has my complete trust. You may speak freely with him in all things. But do it in private."

She nodded.

"You'll need a chaperone, of course. Winifred will do, if you wish."

"Yes. And I want Tobias, too."

He scowled. "Whatever for?"

"Have you some personal objection to Tobias?"

His hands flew up, impatient. "Fine," he said. "By all means, bring Tobias."

She waited a spell for his ruffled feathers to settle before making them rise again.

"Alaric?" she began carefully. "May I ask you a question?"

"I suppose that depends on what it is."

"I know you feel you must marry soon and get yourself an heir, as there is no one left in your family to inherit. What I don't understand is why you must resort to enchantment in order to get yourself a bride. I would think there'd be princesses waiting in line—"

He gripped his head with both hands as if fearing it might come off. "By all the saints in heaven, Molly— is there nothing you will not ask? God's blood, but your impertinence takes my breath away!"

She flushed. "I see I overstepped." And then, because she couldn't help it, "I thought I was your friend."

"Don't," he said, getting up from the bench and going to stand by the pond. He stayed there, not speaking, for an age and more. Then he came back and sat down beside her again.

"It will not be an easy match to make," he said. "When Princess Elizabetta was betrothed to my brother Edmund and came to Dethemere Castle in advance of the marriage, she was in the great hall that night, at my brother's side—"

"I know all that, Alaric. For heaven's sake, I was there."

"Then you will understand that after witnessing the slaughter of my family, including my poor brother whom she was meant to marry—and at such close hand that she was spattered with his very blood—the princess will not look warmly on a match with another king of Westria."

"I agree. It's hopeless. So why not just choose someone else?"

"Because it must be her."

"Oh, come now! She stole your heart in a single day? I know she's beautiful; I saw her myself. But you can't have exchanged a dozen words with the lady. How do you know she's not a shrew, or stupid, or wicked?"

"Neither my heart nor her beauty has anything to do with it, Molly. The kingdom of Cortova controls the Southern Sea. I can't afford to have them turn away from us and make an alliance elsewhere. And there's been talk of a match with Prince Rupert, my cousin Reynard's eldest son."

"That little runt? He can't be more than thirteen!"

"He's fourteen, just two years younger than I; and where royal marriages are concerned, age doesn't matter. If Rupert is matched with Elizabetta, it'll be a disaster for us. Austlind is already allied to Erbano through Reynard's marriage to Beatrice. If they combine with Cortova too, they'll be so powerful, I fear we could not stand against them.

"So I must have an alliance with Cortova. To achieve that, I must wed the princess. And to wed the princess I must, as you so graciously put it, resort to enchantment. Is that clear?"

"As a mountain stream, my lord."

"Good. Now, you'll be going to a crafts town called Faers-Wigan, where your grandfather worked his trade. If one of his cups is still to be had, you should find it there. But I'm a little concerned—"

"—that I won't be able to tell a true cup from a false one?"

He nodded. "There are a lot of dishonest traders who'll be eager to make a sale, and they'll claim—"

"I know. But they won't fool me. I've been seeing

the cup in my dreams this past month and more. I could describe it to you down to the finest detail."

The king brightened upon hearing this. He trusted her magical gift, innocent of the dreadful price she'd paid for the knowledge it brought her. He didn't know—because she'd never told him—how profoundly she dreaded those visions, which came to her unbidden, forcing her to look on unspeakable things. And he certainly couldn't imagine that brash, bold, tough little Molly was haunted by the murder of her grandfather, which she'd witnessed in one of those visions, and the terrible fate of her gentle mother, locked up as a madwoman in a small, dim, noisome room till she was released by death—all because they shared the same magical gift that Molly now carried.

She gazed thoughtfully at the play of water in the pond, thinking not about the cup but the boy who held it: that face, with its straight nose and fine chin, those clear gray eyes, that dark, curly hair—it was like looking into a mirror. He was *herself*, had she been older and a boy.

It had to mean something—that uncanny resemblance, the nightly insistence of the vision. Wouldn't it be wonderful if, just this once, it portended something good?

Best not to count on it, though.

Read the first two books in
DIANE STANLEY'S
thrilling and magical trilogy

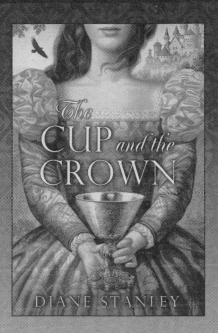

Praise for *The Silver Bowl*:

★ "Stanley succeeds in creating a believable world large enough to accommodate not only menace and evil but also loyalty, enduring friendship, and love." —ALA *Booklist* (starred review)

★ "A most worthy and enjoyable entry in the 'feisty female' fantasy genre." —*Kirkus Reviews* (starred review)

★ "A heroine readers will relate to and cheer for to the satisfying end." —*School Library Journal* (starred review)